VERY TOP SECRET

I finally found the cryonics unit, where they freeze clinically dead people who have enough insurance and the proper papers to be held in cold storage until some brilliant medical genius figured out a way to cure what they *died* from.

A long stainless-steel cylinder was lying on its side, like a section of gleaming sewer pipe. The hose lines leading to it were caked with frost. It looked *cold* in there, colder than Dante's frozen hell.

At the open end of the cylinder ████████ █l table, holding the white, lifeles████████████ e man who had been cover████████████████ y. He was uncovered ████████████████████ usly dead.

My knees sagg████

The dead man ████ James J. Halliday, the President of the United States of America!

"This one will nail your eyebrows to your hairline." —*The Minneapolis Tribune*

Also by Ben Bova
available now from Ballantine Books:

MILLENNIUM

THE
MULTIPLE
MAN

BEN BOVA

A Del Rey Book

BALLANTINE BOOKS • NEW YORK

A Del Rey Book
Published by Ballantine Books

Copyright © 1976 by Ben Bova

All rights reserved including the right of reproduction in whole
or in part in any form. Published in the United States by Ballantine Books, a division of Random House, Inc., New York, and
simultaneously in Canada by Ballantine Books of Canada, Ltd.,
Toronto, Canada.

Library of Congress Catalog Card Number: 75-33505

ISBN 0-345-25656-5

This edition published by arrangement with
The Bobbs-Merrill Company, Inc.

Manufactured in the United States of America

First Ballantine Books Edition: September 1977

Cover art by Joseph Csatari

To Cyrano . . . who could say,
"No, thank you!"

CHAPTER ONE

April is the cruelest month.

It's still winter in Boston. I had tried to get that across to the staff before we left Washington. They had listened, of course, but it never really registered on them. Too excited about the trip. The President didn't make that many public appearances, and they were too busy with the details of this one to worry about top-coats. When we landed at Logan and filed out of the staff plane, that old wind off the harbor knifed right through their doubleweave suits and the women's stylish little jackets. I was the only one with a real coat. Didn't look photogenic, but I didn't freeze my ass, either.

The President didn't seem to notice the cold. While we huddled down on the windswept cement rampway, stamping our feet and blowing on our hands, he stood framed in the hatch of Air Force One, casually smiling and waving for the photographers, while the Secret Service security team set up the laser shields and their other protective paraphernalia. The Man wore only a sport jacket over his turtleneck and slacks. Mr. Casual. When McMurtrie gave him the all-clear nod, he came loping down the ramp in that youthful, long-legged stride of his. The politicians and media flaks surged toward him. The crowds beyond the police lines roared. One of the bands struck up "Hail to the Chief." He smiled and grabbed hands. Everybody smiled back, warm and friendly. Especially the women.

1

"Damn!" Vickie Clark yelled over the noise. "Why didn't you tell me it was going to be this cold?"

"I did." But Vickie's a California girl. She puffed out frigid little clouds of vapor and looked miserable. Which is difficult for her to do. She's an elf, really. Good-looking in a delicate, almost fragile, sort of way. The face of an innocent. With a sharp, tough mind behind it. Vickie typified the White House staff: young, intelligent, an achiever.

Boston is a small city, and the half of it that isn't covered with universities, churches, or historical monuments is covered with politicians. They had all turned out for the President, of course. This was the first time James J. Halliday had been to Boston as President of the United States. We had all swung through twice during last year's campaign, and although the people had come out to see him—pouring into the streets in such numbers, the second time, that the town simply shut down—the politicos had kept a wary distance. Brilliant young governor from the Far West making a dark horse bid for the White House. They were suspicious. They remembered McGovern, way back when, and the aftermath. But now they wanted to show the President that they loved him, and the Federal revenues he represented.

Halliday was in his charming mood. He smiled at everyone, recognized each of those red-faced professional office holders by first name, and just generally went through the airport reception like a combination emperor and movie star. You could feel waves of adulation welling up from the *press,* for God's sake. And the people behind the police security lines were cheering louder than they would for Pat O'Brien's reincarnation. The politicos kept staring and studying The Man with their beady little eyes, trying to figure out what his magic was.

So we had the parade, and the afternoon speech in Boston Common—a cool half-million people overflowed the old park and completely stopped downtown traffic for two hours. ("You should've told me to bring my ski parka," Vickie complained as we stood off to one side of the speaker's platform. I grinned and lent her my topcoat. The sun was shining through the still-bare trees. If The Man could tough it out in a sport jacket, so could I. My coat dropped to Vickie's ankles.)

We rode in the President's limousine to the Boston Sheraton for his press conference. I took the jump seat next to Robert Wyatt, the appointments secretary, and went over the names of the local newsmen with The Man, showing him flash pictures of their faces on the TV viewer built into the limousine's back seat. Halliday had his eidetic memory going; he'd take one look at each picture and have the person's name fixed in his mind.

"I can flash their names on the podium," I told him.

He leaned back in the seat, utterly relaxed. "Might as well. I've got them all up here"—he tapped his temple with a forefinger—"but it's always better to be overequipped than embarrassed."

Robert H. H. Wyatt nodded a tightlipped agreement. Everybody on the staff thought the H. H. stood for "His Holiness." At least, that's what we called him behind his back. He was a crusty old dude, bald, lean, sharp-eyed. Been a retainer of the elder Halliday—the President's father—since before James J. was born. We all felt that one of His Holiness's main duties was to report back to the old man on how and what his son was doing.

Wyatt said, "Mrs. Halliday's due to land at four-fifty; you'll still be at the press conference."

The Man let a flicker of annoyance show. The First Lady had been originally scheduled for an earlier flight, but had begged off for some reason. "You'll have to meet her, Robert, and bring her to the dinner."

Halliday had always been able to handle the Washington press corps like a chess master playing a roomful of amateurs simultaneously. So I wasn't expecting any trouble from the news hounds at the Boston Sheraton. I took a chair in the rear of the ballroom, behind the news and media people and all their cameras and lights, and tried to relax. The Man was enjoying himself up there, making my job easy.

The only sour face in the big ballroom belonged to McMurtrie, who headed the President's security team.

"Relax, Mac," I whispered to him, while Halliday was explaining his stand on the Iranian invasion of Kuwait. "The only danger he's in is from being smothered with affection. These people love him. He's another JFK."

McMurtrie shifted his bulk uneasily, making the folding chair groan. "Nice analogy."

It *was* a stupid thing to say. I tried to retrieve with, "Come on ... you guys've got laser deflectors, riot gas, electric prods, sonic janglers ... it'd take a nuclear bomb to hurt him."

McMurtrie's face looked like a worried Gibraltar. "The Saudis have nukes."

I gave up and leaned back in my chair. Which did not squeak. I'm lanky, but bony.

Up on the podium, under the TV lights, The Man was saying, "Naturally, if Saudi Arabia intervenes, then we will have to assure both the King and the Shah that the United States will remain neutral. We've sold arms freely to both sides. As long as they don't threaten our oil supplies, we can continue to sell them munitions. Short of nuclear weaponry, of course."

One of the women, Betty Turner from *SGR*, jumped to her feet and got the President's nod. "Is that moral, selling arms to both sides?"

Halliday gave her his best grin. "No. It's not. It's not moral to sell weapons or munitions to anyone. But there is no morality in international politics. I found that out long ago. No morality at all. *Except ...*" He let them all dangle on that for a moment. "Except to insure that the best interests of the United States are taken care of. We are still somewhat dependent on both Arabian and Iranian oil, especially since the

Kuwait fields have been temporarily knocked out. In a few years, when we've reached self-sufficiency in energy, we can rethink our Middle Eastern policy. But for the present, if they want to have a war, they're going to do it with our help or without. If we refuse to help them, they will refuse to sell us oil. It's that simple."

Turner opened her mouth for another question, but Halliday went on. "And if we refuse to deal with them, they'll turn elsewhere for help, which is something I don't think we want to see. And, when you get right down to it, if we refuse to deal with either side we will be, de facto, meddling in their internal affairs. As I've said before, our foreign policy is basically very simple ... we are not the world's policeman or the world's pastor. We will do what is best for the United States."

Damn! He didn't go over with that too well. It was phrased too baldly. Goddammit! I'd worked over that foreign policy speech with him for a solid weekend, just the month before, when the Iranians had first jumped into Kuwait. He had bowled over the Washington press corps with what they had described as "shrewd political sense and uncommon candor." You'd think he could remember the goddamned wording. It's all-important in this game; it's not merely what you say, it's the way you say it. You can carry candor too far.

McMurtrie nudged me gently with his elbow. For a guy his size, "gently" can leave your ribs sore. "Now *you* look worried." He came as close as he ever does to smiling. "Welcome to the club."

I had begged off attending the dinner before we'd left Washington. The First Lady flew into Logan late in the afternoon and met Halliday at the hotel. Then they went off to their quiet little thousand-buck-a-plate dinner at the Harvard Club. I kept wondering what old Harry Truman would've said to *that*.

Vickie covered the dinner for me, letting old Wyatt escort her. It was unusual to see her so dressed up, in a long gown and everything. With her slim figure, she looked like a high-schooler going to her first prom. But she had good color sense; her gown was sea-green, and it picked up the color of her eyes while setting off her sunstreaked blonde hair beautifully.

His Holiness looked stunning in an old-fashioned tuxedo. His parchment-smooth face glistened; he had reached the age where his skin had taken on that translucent look that only infants and octogenarians have. He made a stately old gentlemanly figure. Vickie could have been his granddaughter, making her debut in society.

I assured them both that I'd show up for The Man's speech in Faneuil Hall at nine, and they left for the Harvard Club. I debated with myself for a moment when I got to the hotel lobby, then decided to walk to my own dinner appointment.

It had been only a little more than two years since I'd left Boston to join Halliday's campaign and eventually become a member of his White House staff. The city hadn't changed much. A couple of new towers going up in Back Bay, their gaunt skeletons outlined against the dusk. The same gaggles of students in their raunchy Guccis and carefully scuffed sneakers, out looking for an evening's fun. The same chill wind that cut through you, no matter how heavy a coat you wore.

I walked briskly through the deepening shadows, watched the evening star duck in and out behind the buildings, and refrained from making any wishes. I felt cold, alone, and suddenly damned bitter. I was heading for the North End, to have dinner with an old newspaper buddy, and the past couple of years were unreeling in my mind like a rerun of a TV documentary. I should have been proud of every minute of it. It should have been a great time in my life. No one except me knew that it wasn't. At least, that's what I thought and hoped.

There's a particular rhythm to a city, different for each one. After so many months in Washington, which is really a Southern town with ulcers, I could tell that I was in Boston even with my eyes closed. The chaotic snarl of traffic, with each driver making damned certain King George III won't tell *him* which side of the street he could drive on. The anguished nasal bleat of the improper Bostonian telling his neighbor to "Have a haaaht, willya?" or "Open th'doah, fir the luvva God!"

It was fully dark by the time I got to the North End. The street market around Faneuil Hall, on the other side of the expressway overhead, was closing down. So were the store owners in Little Italy, taking in their sidewalk wares. Still, there was an aroma of spices and olives, and the sound of old men playing *morre* under the shadow of Paul Revere's Old North Church spire. It made me incredibly homesick.

Johnny Harrison was halfway through a water tumbler of red wine when I stepped into Rita's. The place hadn't changed at all. It was tiny, actually just the front room of a private house. Only six little booths. Linoleum floor covering. Steam radiators hissing and making the place almost uncomfortably warm. Paintings of Naples and Venice by one of the neighborhood kids fading on the walls. Conchetta, the waitress, still bleaching her hair in the hope that it would make her glamorous. Kitchen in the next room.

You had to know Rita's existed in order to find the place. The entrance was on an alley that used to be blocked all the time by a Mafiosi Cadillac. Now it was an electric Mercedes. Word of mouth was the only advertising that Rita went in for, and most of it was in Italian.

There's a vague air of Groucho Marx about Johnny Harrison. Maybe it's because he's an old movie buff. He always looks as if he knows more than you do, and he's always got a quip ready. He'd put on some weight in the year or so since I'd last seen him, but I knew that if I mentioned it, he'd spill out a string of skinny jokes about me. Besides, sitting next to him was a stranger, a compact young soccer-player type who had the eager puppy dog look of a new reporter all over him.

I slid into the booth. "Hiya, Johnny."

He made a grin. "I was starting to wonder if you'd show up."

Three minutes late. I didn't bother answering that one.

"This here's Len Ryan," Johnny said. "He'll be covering the President's speech tonight from the local angle. Y'know ... historic Faneuil Hall, where Sam Adams's patriots put on their Indian disguises for the Boston Tea Party, was the scene tonight of another grrreat moment in American democracy . . ."

Ryan clapped his hand to his head. "May my typewriter blow a fuse if I ever write crap like that!"

We all laughed. Then Johnny got just a little formal. "Leonard, me lad, this is Meric Albano, the press secretary to the President of the United States. One of my proteges. We started together on the old *Globe,* and have spent many a lonely dinner hour right in this very booth."

Ryan extended his hand. "An honor, Mr. Albano."

His grip was very muscular. "Meric," I told him.

"Americo," Johnny said. "The son of an overly patriotic would-be poet."

"My father was a civil engineer," I said. "I was born the day he and my mother landed here."

"In Boston?" Ryan asked.

"No. Cleveland. The flight was supposed to land in Boston, but a snowstorm had closed Logan. We got to Boston on a bus, finally."

"Three weeks later," Johnny said. "A fascinating beginning to a fascinating life."

"I've been very fortunate," I kidded.

"And we are honored," Johnny went on, "that you could pull yourself away from your duties to break bread with us."

"And bend elbows," I said.

"Indeed." He took his glass in hand, squinted at the

reflections of the overhead bulbs in the red wine, then realized that I didn't have anything to drink. He signaled to Conchetta, who nodded and smiled hello at me.

Dinner was pleasant enough, except when Johnny's bantering got around to Laura.

"She did arrive okay, didn't she?" he asked.

"Yes. They're having dinner at the Harvard Club."

"Laura?" Ryan asked. "You mean the First Lady?"

"Indeed so," Johnny said, twirling a forkful of linguini like an expert. "Laura Benson and Meric were childhood sweethearts . . ."

"Hardly childhood," I said, trying to keep the anger from showing. "She was in Radcliffe and I was going to Boston University."

Johnny shrugged good-naturedly, without losing a single strand of linguini. "At any rate, they went through all the pangs of True Love. Except that somehow she ended up marrying the Governor of Colorado."

"Who is now the President," Ryan finished.

"Exactly. And our dear friend Meric, here . . . stalwart, steady, duty-first Meric, ends up as the President's press secretary. And I am naught but a lowly city editor. Strange world. And to think I taught him everything he knows, too. Do you get to see much of her, Meric?"

My mouth dodged the issue before my brain could think it over. "Why do you think I'm having dinner here with you guys tonight?"

Ryan tagged along with me as I walked through the underpasses beneath the expressway to Faneuil Hall. The night was turning colder, getting cloudy. The youngster seemed to be goggle-eyed at the idea of being among Great Men. I didn't disillusion him, although Johnny's wine-soaked probing had left a sour feeling in my gut.

The auditorium inside Faneuil Hall had just been redecorated from floor to ceiling. As always in Boston, there had been a titanic argument over whether the motif should be Original Puritan, Patriotic Colonial, or Bullfinch Federalist. The patriots won, and the place looked stately and elegant in that Colonial blend of severity and warmth. Blues and golds dominated, with natural wood tones gleaming here and there.

The place was jammed with the Massachusetts research and development intelligentsia. Scientists from MIT and Harvard, engineers from the once-magical Route 128 "electronic highway," the survivors of booms and busts that had staggered the R & D industry and the nation's economy with the regularity of a major league slugger taking batting practice.

I didn't have anything to do with his speech. Robinson and the other speechwriters put it together, although The Man always put a lot of pure Halliday into everything he said. And he tied the speech into the afternoon press conference's questions about the Iranian war in an ad-lib way that no speechwriter can prepare ahead of time:

". . . the real issue is very clear. The basic question is survival. Survival for the way of life we have worked so hard to achieve. Survival for the democratic institutions that have made us a great and prosperous people. Survival for our children and our children's children.

"We can no longer allow ourselves to be dependent on dwindling natural resources for the primary needs of our people. Nor need we be so dependent, when we have within our grasp—thanks to the dedication and perseverance of our nation's scientists and engineers— new sources of energy that will eliminate forever the twin dangers that haunt us: resource depletion and pollution of the environment.

"It is my intention, and I am sure the Congress will agree, to push ahead for the development of new energy systems, such as the orbiting solar network and the laser-fusion generators, with all the vigor that we can command."

They loved it. For the first time in their memories a President was treating them like an important national resource. It meant huge dollops of Federal money for the brainboys, sure. But more important to that audience on that night was the fact that the President, The Man himself, was saying to them, "We need you, we want you, we admire you." They would have followed him anywhere, just as their fathers had followed Kennedy to the moon.

But he seemed stiff to me. Uncomfortable. He was *reading* the speech, something he almost never did. Only an insider would notice it, I figured, but he looked to me as if he weren't really all that familiar with the speech.

Laura was sitting on the stage, just to the right of the podium, looking more beautiful than ever. The lime-light of attention and public homage seemed to be making her more self-assured, more pleased with herself and the world around her. She was a goddess whose worshipers were a nation. They knew it and she knew it. So she sat there, smiling, beautiful, adored, and remote. From me.

I pulled my attention away from her and let my eyes wander across the rapt audience. I wondered what Sam Adams and his roughnecks would have to say about this crowd. How many of these well-dressed heavily educated people would daub red clay on their faces and dress in Indian feathers to go out and defy the laws of the Government? A few, I guessed. Damned few. And I wasn't certain I could count myself among them.

The whole stage, up where the President and his group were, was protected by an invisible laser-actuated shield. And there were other, redundant, shields around the podium and the body of the President. If anyone tried to fire a shot from the audience, the scanning lasers would pick up the bullet in flight and zap it into vapor with a microsecond burst of energy. Sonic janglers would paralyze everyone in the auditorium, and McMurtrie's men could pick up the would-be assassin at their leisure. Foolproof quantum-electronic security. All done with the speed of light. The President could appear to be standing alone and in the open, naked to his enemies, when he was actually protected so well that no major assassinations had been successful in years.

Which is why I was more startled than annoyed when McMurtrie grabbed my shoulder and whispered, subtle as a horse, "Follow me."

I didn't have much choice. He had already half-lifted me out of my seat in the press section. Len Ryan glanced at me quizzically. It must have looked like I was being hauled off on a drug bust.

"I'll be right back," I mouthed at him as McMurtrie practically dragged me to the nearest exit.

He waited for the big metal door to close fully before he said, "We've got troubles, and you've got to keep the news hounds out of it."

Framed by the bare-walled exit tunnel that led to the alley, lit from above by a single unshielded bulb, McMurtrie looked troubled indeed. His big beefy face was a map of worry and brooding belligerence.

"What's happened?" I asked. "What's the matter . . ."

He shook his head and grabbed my arm. Leading me down the tunnel toward the outside door, which opened onto the alley behind the Hall, he said only, "Don't ask questions. Just keep the news people off our backs. We can't have a word leak out about this. Understand? Not word number one."

And his grip on my arm was squeezing so hard that my hand started to go numb.

"It would help if . . ."

He barged through the outside fire door and we were out in the alley. It was cold. The wind was cutting and there were even a few flakes of snow swirling in the light cast by the bulb over the door. I wished for my topcoat, silently, because McMurtrie was dragging me up the alley, away from the street and into the deeper shadows, and he wasn't going to give me a chance to even ask for the damned coat.

The alley angled right, and as we turned the bend I saw a huddle of people bending over something. Two of them wore Boston police uniforms. The other half-dozen were in civvies. They had that Secret Service no-nonsense look about them.

McMurtrie didn't have to push through them. They parted as he approached. What they were bending over was a blanket. Lying there on the pavement of this dirt-encrusted alley. A blanket with a body under it. I could see a pair of shoes poking out from the blanket's edge.

"The doctor here yet?" McMurtrie asked gruffly.

One of the Secret Service agents answered, "On his way, sir."

"Both ends of this alley sealed?"

"Yessir. Four men at each end. Ambulance . . ."

"No ambulance. No noise. Get one of our cars. Call Klienerman; tell him to meet us at Mass General."

"He's still in Washington, isn't . . . ?"

"Get him up here on an Air Force jet." McMurtrie turned to another security man. "You get to Mass General and have them clear out the cryonics facility. Screen the place yourself. Take as many men as you need from the local FBI office. *Move.*"

The agent scampered like a scared freshman.

I was still staring at the shoes. *Who the hell would be walking around back here?* The shoes looked brand new, not a bum's.

McMurtrie had turned to the two Boston cops. "Would you mind securing the fire door, up the alley? No one in or out until we get this cleared away." He barely gestured toward the body.

The cops nodded. They were both young and looked scared.

Then McMurtrie fixed me with a gun-metal stare. "You'd better go back inside the way you came out. Make sure the press people stay in there to the end of the President's speech. Do not let any of them out here."

"How can I keep . . ."

He laid a stubby finger against my chest. It felt as if it weighed half a ton. "I don't care how you do it. Just do it. Then meet us at the Mass General cryonics facility after the speech. Alone. No reporters."

He was dead serious. And the man under the blanket was dead. My brain began to whirl. It couldn't be an assassination attempt. One well-shod character staggers into an alley to have a heart attack and McMurtrie acts as if we're being invaded by Martians.

But I didn't argue. I went back to the fire door, a couple of steps behind the two cops. Maybe McMurtrie was just overreacting. Or maybe, crafty son of a bitch that he was, he was using this accident as an opportunity to test his troops' capabilities.

Sure, that's it. A practice run, courtesy of a wino whose time ran out. I was about to smile when the rest of my brain asked, *Then why's he bringing Dr. Klienerman up from Washington? And what's he want the Massachusetts General Hospital's cryonics facility for? He's going to dip the wino in liquid nitrogen and make a frozen popsicle out of him?*

One look at the faces of those two Boston patrolmen drove all the levity out of me. They were *scared*. Not from finding a wino in an alley. Not from brushing against the President's security team. Something was in their eyes that I hadn't seen since the San Fernando quake—these guys were terrified of something that went beyond human control.

They had reached the fire door a few paces ahead of me and turned to stand guard. I stopped when they looked at me. One of them had his electric prod in his gloved hands. The other had hooked his thumb around the butt of his revolver.

"Uh . . . McMurtrie told me to go back inside," I mumbled. Somehow I felt guilty in their eyes.

"Yeah, we heard him." That's all either one of them

said. One of them opened the fire door and I stepped back inside the Hall.

I was shaking. And not entirely from the cold.

The President's speech was almost over as I took my seat.

"What happened?" Ryan whispered to me. "You look awful."

I tried giving him a fierce glance. "Just cold. I'm okay."

"What's going on?"

"Nothing," I lied. "McMurtrie wanted to check the arrangements for the President's ride back to Logan. Wanted to know if I had planned a Q and A session after the speech."

Ryan looked a bit puzzled, but he apparently accepted that. I felt lucky that he was a local reporter and not one of the Washington corps, who know that we never have a question period following a speech. Especially when The Man's already given a press conference the same day.

Halliday wound up his speech, the audience cheered mightily, and the usual round of handshaking started up on stage. The Hall emptied slowly, although most of the reporters raced for the nearest exits to get back to their offices and file their stories. The few who tried to take an alley exit were turned back, grumbling.

Ryan didn't leave, though.

"Don't you have a deadline to meet?" I asked him as we walked slowly toward the back of the Hall, following the emptying throng.

He paced alongside me, stubborn faced and tweedy. "I'm doing the color piece for the afternoon edition. Got plenty of time. I was wondering ... Johnny thought it might be fun to do an interview with you."

"Me?"

"Sure." He waved an arm in the air. "Local man makes good. What it's like to work in the White House. The inside story of the most popular President since Roosevelt . . . that kind of stuff."

"Not now," I said. "I've got to join the rest of the staff and get back to Washington. No time for an interview."

"Too bad."

I didn't like the look on his face: more curious than disappointed. Or maybe I was projecting.

"Look," I said. "Why don't we do the interview by phone. Give me a call early next week and we'll set up a time. Okay?"

He nodded without smiling. "Sure."

Ryan offered me a ride to the airport, once we got outside to the windy, cold street. I told him I was going to ride in one of the staff limousines; it was all set up. He took it with an air of dubious graciousness, shook my hand, and jogged off through the shadows to the parking lot. I watched the wind pluck at his coat.

There was one cab left in front of Faneuil Hall, and I felt damned lucky to get it. I ducked inside, glad to be out of the wind.

"Mass General," I told the cabbie.

"Ya know how t'get there?" he asked from the other side of his bulletproof shield.

"Damned right I do!" I snapped. Boston cabbies have sent their kids to Harvard on the meter readings of their excursions. The city is small, but no two streets connect in any logical way. You could spend two hours circling your destination if you didn't know where it was.

I gave the cabbie detailed instructions on how to get there. His only response was a grumbling, "Awright, awright," as he snapped the meter flag down and put the taxi in gear.

Any large hospital is a maze of haphazard corridors, buildings joined together in an unplanned sprawl of growth, cloying smells of medicine and fear and pain. It makes me nervous just to visit a sick friend.

I finally found the cryonics unit, where they freeze clinically dead people who have enough insurance and the proper papers to be held in cold storage until some brilliant medical genius figures out a way to cure what they "died" from.

It looked more like something out of NASA than a hospital facility. Lots of stainless steel, metal desks, and computer consoles lining the walls. Everything painted white, like a clean-room facility. Fluorescent panels in the ceiling overhead cast a glareless, shadowless light that somehow made me edgy, nervous. One whole wall of the main room was a long window. At first glance I thought it was an operating "theater" on the other side.

McMurtrie was sitting at one of the desks, outbulking it and looking grimly ominous. A covey of green-smocked hospital people worked at the other desks. The computer was humming to itself, lights flickering on its read-out console as if it were telling itself a good joke. McMurtrie's agents were standing around, looking uneasy and suspicious.

As I stepped in, I realized that McMurtrie was talking to someone on the picture-phone. The tiny screen on the desk top showed a middle-aged man who looked rather rumpled and unhappy.

"I'm very sorry to have to bother you at this hour, Dr. Klienerman," McMurtrie was rumbling in a tone as close to politeness as I've ever heard from him. "If you agree to freezing the body we can transport it back to Walter Reed and have it ready for your examination in the morning."

Klienerman said something, but I didn't hear it. My eye had caught the scene inside the cryonics "theater."

A long stainless-steel cylinder was lying on its side, like a section of gleaming sewer pipe. All around it were blue-painted tanks of liquid nitrogen, with lines leading from them into the cylinder. The hose lines were caked with frost, and steamy white vapor was eddying out of the cylinder's open end. It looked *cold* in there; colder than Dante's frozen hell.

At the open end of the cylinder was a hospital table, holding the whitely lifeless body of a man. The man who had been covered by the blanket in the alley behind Faneuil Hall. He was uncovered now. Completely naked. Obviously dead.

My knees sagged beneath me.

The dead man was James J. Halliday, the President of the United States of America.

CHAPTER TWO

It was McMurtrie who grabbed me. He wrapped his gorilla arms around my shoulders. Otherwise I would've gone right down to the floor.

"It's not *him*," he whispered fiercely. "It's a copy, a duplicate . . ."

I was having trouble breathing. Everything seemed to be out of focus, blurred. I couldn't get air into my lungs.

Next thing I knew I was sitting down and gulping at a plastic cup's worth of water. McMurtrie was looming over me. But I was still looking past him, at the body lying in the cryonics chamber. Cold. Dead.

"It's not the President," McMurtrie said at me. "He's on the plane, on his way back to Washington. I talked to him ten minutes ago." He jerked a thumb toward the picture-phone on the desk.

"Then who . . ." My voice sounded weak and cracked, as if it were coming from someone else, somebody old and badly scared.

McMurtrie shook his head, like a buffalo getting rid of gnats. "Damned if I know. But we'll find out. Believe it."

I was beginning to register normally again. Taking a deep breath, I straightened up in the chair and looked around the glareless white room. Four of McMurtrie's men were standing around. They had nothing to do, but they looked alert and ready. One of them, closest to the door, had his pistol out and was minutely examining the action, clicking it back and forth. The ammo clip was tucked into his jacket's breast pocket.

"Somebody's made a double for the President," I said to McMurtrie, with some strength in my voice now, "and your men killed him."

He glared at me. "No such thing. We found this ... man ... in the alley. Just where you saw him. He was dead when those two cops stumbled over him. No identification. No marks of violence."

I thought about that for a moment. "Just lying there stretched out in the alley."

"The cops thought he was a drunk, except he was dressed too well. Then when they saw his face ..."

"No bullet wounds or needle marks or anything?"

McMurtrie said, "Go in there and examine him yourself, if you want to."

"No, thanks." But I found myself staring at the corpse in the misty cold chamber. He looked *exactly* like Halliday.

"Are you in good enough shape to walk?" McMurtrie asked me.

"I guess so."

"And talk?"

It was my turn to glare at him. "What do you think I'm doing now?"

He grinned. It was what he did instead of laughing. "There're a few reporters out at the front desk. The local police and two of my people are keeping them there. Somebody's going to have to talk to them."

I knew who somebody was. "What do I tell them? Disneyland's made a copy of the President?"

"You don't tell them a damned thing," McMurtrie said. "But you send them home satisfied that they know why we're here. Got it?"

I nodded. "Give 'em the old Ziegler shuffle. Sure. I'll walk on water, too. Just to impress them."

He leaned over so that his face was close enough for me to smell his mouth freshener. "Listen to me. This is *important*. We cannot have the media finding out that there was an exact duplicate of the President running loose in Boston tonight."

"He wasn't exactly running loose," I said.

"Not one word about it."

"What'd he die of?"

He shrugged massively. "Don't know. Our own medical people gave him a quick going over, but there's no way to tell yet. We're going to freeze him and ship him down to Klienerman at Walter Reed."

"Before I talk to the reporters," I said, "I want to check with The Man."

McMurtrie grumbled just enough to stay in character, then let me use the phone. It took only a few moments to get through on the special code to the President in Air Force One. They were circling Andrews AFB, about to land. But one thing the President insists on is instant communications, wherever he is. He's never farther away from any of his staff than the speed of light.

In the tiny screen of the desk-top phone, he looked a little drawn. Not tired or worried so much as nettled, almost angry. I reviewed the situation with him very quickly.

"And McMurtrie thinks I ought to stonewall the reporters," I concluded.

His public smile was gone. His mouth was tight. "What do you think?" he asked me.

One of Halliday's tenets of faith had been total honesty with the press. He was damned fair to the working news people, which is one of the reasons I was attracted to him in the first place. Completely aside from Laura.

"I'm afraid he's right, Mr. President," I answered. "We can't let this out . . . not right now."

"Why not?"

It was a question he always asked. Working for him was a constant exercise in thinking clearly. "Because"— I thought as clearly and fast as I could—"a disclosure now would raise more questions than answers. Who is this . . . this double? How'd he get to look like you? And why? How did he die? And . . ." I hesitated.

He caught it. "And is it really James J. Halliday you've got cooling down in there, while I'm an imposter replacing him? Right?"

I had to agree. "That's the biggie. And if you're an imposter, who're you working for?"

He grinned. "The Republicans."

Seriously, he asked, "Meric . . . do you think I'm an imposter?"

"Not for a microsecond."

"Why not?"

"You wouldn't be challenging me like this if you were. Besides, you're behaving exactly the way you always behave."

He cocked his head to one side slightly, which is another of his personal little pieces of action. I had never paid much attention to it until that moment.

"All right," he said at last. "I don't like hiding things from the press unless there's a damned vital reason for it."

"This is very vital," I said.

He agreed and then asked to speak with McMurtrie. I got up from the desk and stared again into the cold chamber. The team of green-gowned meditechs was starting to slide the corpse into the stainless-steel cylinder that would be his cryonic sarcophagus. Liquid nitrogen boil-off filled the chamber with whitish vapor. Each of the meditechs wore a face mask; I'd never be able to identify them again.

Then that one word struck me. *Exactly*. The man I had just spoken to on the picture-phone acted exactly like the James J. Halliday I'd known and worked for since he first started campaigning. The corpse they were sliding into that cold metal cylinder looked exactly like James J. Halliday. My knees got fluttery again.

McMurtrie came over beside me. I could see our two reflections in the glass that separated us from the cold chamber. He looked as grim as vengeance. I looked scared as shit.

"Okay, kid," he told me. "You're in the big leagues now. Put on a straight face and get those newsmen out of here while we ship the casket out the back way."

One of his men walked with me up to the waiting room near the hospital's main entrance. He was a typical McMurtrie trooper: neatly dressed, quiet and colorless to the point of invisibility. And perfectly capable of quietly, colorlessly, maybe even bloodlessly, killing a man. It was something to think about.

Len Ryan was among the news people in the waiting room. There were eleven of them, a modern baker's dozen, sitting on the worn and tired-looking plastic chairs, talking and joking with one another when I walked in. Ryan was off in a corner by himself, writing in a thick notebook. He threw me a look that was halfway between suspicion and contempt.

"Don't any of the news chicks in this town work late anymore?" I cracked, putting on my professional smile.

"They were all at the airport interviewing the First Lady," said the guy nearest me. He was grossly overweight, not the type you'd expect to chase ambulances. I hadn't known him when I'd worked for the *Globe,* but he looked older than I. New in town, I figured.

It was a small room. I stepped into it a few paces and they all stood up expectantly. The floor tiles had been patterned once, but now the colors were all but obliterated from years of people's frightened, weary pacing. The lights were too bright. The heat was up too high. Through the two sealed windows I could see cars whizzing by on Storrow Drive, and the river beyond them, and MIT beyond the river. I wished I could be out there someplace, anyplace, away from here.

"What's going on, Meric?" asked Max Freid of UPI. We used to call him "Hotdog Max," because he was always shooting for the spectacular story. "Why all the hustle with the Secret Service? Who's the stiff?"

"Take it easy," I said, making slowdown motions with my hands. "Don't get yourselves excited. Apparently some wino staggered into the alley behind Faneuil Hall tonight and keeled over from a heart attack." *McMurtrie can arrange with the local FBI office to slip a real wino who really died tonight into the Mass General files.* "The police patrolling the area found him and alerted the President's security team. They are very protective guys, as you may have noticed, and they had the body shipped here immediately. Just routine precaution, that's all." *Better get those two Boston patrolmen sent to Washington or otherwise put on ice. If these wiseasses get their hands on them, the story'll pop out in fifteen minutes. The meditechs were Army people, from what McMurtrie said. Check on it.*

"Seems like a helluva lot of overreaction for one dead wino."

I nodded at them. "Yeah. I suppose so. But that's the way these security people react. Nobody's hit a President—or even a candidate—in a lot of years. Right?" *What about tonight? Was it an attempt? Did it succeed?*

They muttered reluctant agreement.

"Listen, fellas." Now I had to throw the strikeout pitch. "I spoke to the President on the phone just before I came over here. I suggested, and he agreed, that I ask you guys not to print anything about this little incident . . ."

"I knew it!"

"Come on, Meric. For Chri . . ."

"Hear me out!" I raised my voice. When they stopped grumbling, I went on. "I don't like to ask you to do this, and the President was even more hesitant . . ."

"Then why ask?" It came from Len Ryan.

"Simply because it *was* just a harmless incident that shouldn't be blown up out of proportion. And because everytime there's been a news story that even hints at an assassination attempt, every kook in the country turns violent. You know that. I don't have to tell you about it."

"What about the President's terrific security team? Are they scared of a little exercise?"

"Wise up!" I snapped. "The Man's got the best protection in the world. But why *invite* trouble? Why put the idea in some nut's head? Because a drunk dropped dead in an alley? Come off it."

"How'd he get back there? Wasn't there a police net around the Hall?"

That's right, I realized. *How the hell did he get into that alley?* But my mouth was getting very clever. "That's just my point. No security system is perfect. Thank God it was just a harmless drunk."

"I'll have to ask my city editor about this," said one of the men in the back of the room. "We can't guarantee not to print it."

"Listen! Remember the attempt on Jackson's life, back in the eighties?"

"The poor slob never got within a hundred yards of Jackson . . ."

"Sure," I said. "But the following week that mental patient killed eleven people in Sacramento, right? And the sniper in Dayton, right after that?"

"You can't prove that a news story made them go berserk."

"I don't have to prove it," I said. "I just want you guys, and your editors, to understand what's at stake here. You make a story out of this incident and you might set off a new Boston Strangler."

"Jesus Christ!" somebody muttered. "Might as well blame us for Jack the Ripper."

It took a lot more talk. And phone calls to a half-dozen sleepy, short-tempered editors. I called right from the hospital's main switchboard, while they clustered around me. It was past two in the morning when the last one of them agreed to sit on the story.

I was dead tired. The reporters filed out of the hospital, too frustrated to complain about spending the night for nothing.

"Still going to the airport in an official limousine?"

It was Ryan. He was the last one left, as I stood in the hospital's entrance corridor. Nobody else there except him and me, and the near-invisible security man leaning his back against the wall.

"I stalled you," I admitted. "I'm sorry about it. They found a corpse in the alley and everybody got a little fidgety."

He nodded, a compact little jerk of his head. He had a bull neck and looked as if he could be very stubborn when he wanted to be. And idealistic. He reminded me of myself at that age. Maybe that's why I didn't like him.

"I can still drive you to the airport," he said.

"No. Thanks, anyway. I wouldn't want to take you out of your way. I've asked enough of you for one night."

That brought a smile out of him. "It's on my way. My pad's in Winthrop. Come on . . . you look beat."

Reluctantly, I let him lead me out to the parking lot and I got into his car. Ryan didn't say a word while we drove to the airport. I must have dozed for a few minutes. The next thing I remember is pulling up in front of the terminal building where the staff jet was still parked.

"Thanks for the lift," I said as I started to haul myself out of the Toyota Electric.

"Any time."

Being careful not to bump my head, I finally squeezed out onto the sidewalk, like the last drop of toothpaste coming out of a rolled-up tube. Ducking back inside, I shook Ryan's extended hand.

"I'll call you in a couple of days," he said. "I think I'd like to come to Washington to interview you. Now."

I banged my head on the door top as I pulled away from him.

There were several strange men trying to look inconspicuous as they guarded the terminal entrances, the corridor, and the ramp gate near the staff plane. FBI, I assumed. They didn't have the air of McMurtrie's people.

The plane was warm and comfortable and filled with sleeping people. Most of the staff had been inside all night, since The Man's speech ended. The lights were so dim I could barely make out their sleeping forms, curled up or stretched out in the plush swivel seats.

McMurtrie wasn't asleep, though. He was sitting up forward, with a tiny worklight making his seat and folding table an island of wakefulness in the darkened plane. I went up to him and saw that he was doing nothing, just sitting there and staring off into infinity.

The engines began to whine into life. The seat-belt sign flashed on. I took the chair next to McMurtrie, leaned across the space separating us, and asked, "Anything new?"

He shook his head silently.

"Do they"—I hooked a thumb back toward the rest of the staff—"know about it?"

It was obvious that I was breaking into his private chain of thought. He turned slowly toward me and rumbled, "So far we've been able to keep it from them. There's no sense spreading this any further than it has to go."

I agreed. "Where's the, uh, capsule? The cryonic container?"

"On a separate plane, heading for Minnesota."

I blinked at him. "Where?"

"A special laboratory in Minnesota. The President's orders. We're flying Dr. Klienerman out there tomorrow. Be easier to maintain security that way."

By *security* he meant *secrecy*.

"The President told you to do that?"

McMurtrie nodded.

"Himself?"

He nodded again, but with growing impatience.

"It wasn't Wyatt or one of the other staffers? It was The Man himself, personally?"

McMurtrie never loses his self-control. He thinks. But he's not accustomed to being interrogated. "Yes, it was the President himself," he said, keeping his voice so low that I could barely hear it over the rising roar of the plane's engines. "Exactly the same procedure as before."

Even through my sleepy, foggy brain that last word hit me. "Before? What before?"

For just a flash of a second he realized he'd said something he shouldn't have. He reached out and clamped a heavy hand around my arm. "Keep your voice down, damn you!"

"This has happened before?" I insisted. "This isn't the first time?"

His face contorted with barely suppressed rage, McMurtrie answered, "Ask the President about it. Not me."

"I will," I snapped at him. "I sure as hell will!"

CHAPTER THREE

It should have seemed like a bad dream the next morning. I awoke with the sunlight streaming through my bedroom window. Rock Creek Park was green and leafy out there. In Washington, April is almost summertime. The cherry trees were in bloom along the Tidal Basin and up Fourteenth Street. The sky was clear and bright blue.

But I still felt lousy. Not just from having only a few hours' sleep. I was scared.

None of the staff had offices in the White House anymore. Even though Halliday kept a very small staff, compared to any President since Truman, he still insisted on keeping the White House exclusively to himself. Why he and Laura needed the entire executive mansion was the object of a lot of snide talk in Washington. It had been a source of smutty jokes during the first few months of Halliday's Administration. But then he began hitting his stride as President and started giving people the best damned government they'd had in a generation. The jokes died away. As the stock market climbed, inflation leveled off, and some headway was made even on the stubborn unemployment figures, jokes about Halliday went from nasty to nice. He was beloved by all.

But he still wouldn't let any of us set up shop in the White House. Security was the unspoken byword. Thinking back on all the Presidents and candidates who'd been shot over the years, who could blame him?

It seemed to be his only quirk; he was damned tight about his personal security. And privacy.

Every morning, for example, I went through our daily press briefing on the phone with The Man. I sat in my office and we reviewed the day's news over the picture-phone. Then I'd go down and give the morning briefing to the Washington press corps. I hardly ever went to the White House. None of us did. We talked with the President through the picture-phones. Some days he was light and jovial. Some days he was tense and critical. Once or twice he was downright bitchy at us, especially when we had to face bad economic news. But it was a very rare day when he asked one of us to the White House for a face-to-face discussion. "We all work for the phone company," was a common song in our offices.

The staff was housed in offices in the buildings right around the White House. Mine was in the Aztec Temple. We called it that because it was heated and cooled entirely by solar energy, a demonstration project of the Energy Research and Development Agency. It was shaped like a stepped-back pyramid, to make as many sun-catching surfaces as possible. And it worked pretty well, too, except that the place got chillier than hell in deep winter. And the slightest covering of snow shut down the solar panels completely. We got more snow holidays than the local school kids did.

My office was cool and dry when I got into it; the air conditioning was working fine. But I barely noticed. While Greta brought me my morning coffee and situation reports, and made her usual motherly noises about the bags under my eyes and getting the sleep I need, I punched the phone keyboard.

It takes a few minutes to go up the White House ladder, even for the President's press secretary. I leaned back in my desk chair, flicked on the network channels on five of the TV screens that made the far wall of my office look like an insect's eye, and took a cautious sip of the steaming black coffee.

Sure enough, I burned my tongue. All five of the

morning news programs were talking about things other than last night's excitement in Boston. I had the sound off, of course. Some of the electronics smart boys had rigged the screens with print-outs that spelled out what the people on the screens were mouthing. I often thought that if everybody's home TV worked that way, without the noise, we'd all be a lot saner.

The newscasters were showing the latest fighting in Kuwait, complete with sky-high pillars of oily black smoke making a damned expensive background for the Shah's air-cushion armored personnel carriers. Then they all switched to the President's speech in Boston. But not one word about the body in the alley.

Robert H. H. Wyatt appeared on my phone screen.

"Good morning, Meric. How are you today?"

"Rotten," I told him. "I've got to see The Man. Now. If not sooner."

Nothing ever surprised or ruffled old Robert. He sat there for a moment, and the only thing happening to convince you he wasn't a wax statue was the barely detectable throbbing of a bluish vein in his gleaming bald head.

"You'll have your regular news review at . . ."

"Robert," I snapped, "turn your scrambler on, please."

He blinked once, and I saw his shoulders move. His hands were out of the screen's view. I flicked on the scrambler at my end, and the little phone screen flickered briefly. Then the picture steadied again.

Before His Holiness could say anything, I popped, "Robert, you know what happened last night."

"Last night?"

To hell with it. I knew he knew. I was certain of it. He's closer to the President than McMurtrie or me or any of his staffers. He's the President's surrogate father, for Christ's sake.

"A body was found in the alley behind Faneuil Hall. It looked exactly like James J. Halliday. I mean *exactly*. And it's not the first time it's happened, either."

His face went dead white. Wyatt had never seemed too strong; he was frail and slow-moving, and he always had a pale, waxy look to him. But the last hint of color drained from his face. His left eye ticked uncontrollably, several times.

"Last night, you say?" His voice was barely audible.

"You didn't know about it?"

"Not this one."

"I've got to see the President," I said again. "This is too big to keep out of the news indefinitely. If there's a plot to slip a double into his place . . . or if they've already . . ."

"They?" The strength flowed back into him. He frowned at me. "What do you mean *they?*"

"How the hell do I know? The Russians. The Chinese. The Saudis. Somebody's trying to get a man who looks exactly like the President into places where the President is. Who and why?"

He said firmly, "That's a matter for the internal security people, not the press secretary."

I made my voice as stubborn as his. "Robert, sooner or later I'm going to have to either tell what I know to the press, or try to hide this from them. I won't act in the dark; I'm not going to be a trained parrot. I want to see The Man this morning. I want to make sure that he's the same man I agreed to work for."

His mouth opened, but no words came out. Not for several seconds. Finally he glanced down for a moment, then looked back at me and said, "Eleven forty-five. The Vice-President will be in with him, too, but I suppose it's a matter that you should participate in with them. And then you can stay for a few minutes after the Vice-President leaves."

I nodded. "Oval Office?"

"Yes."

Visitors to the White House go in through the East Wing and are guided past the showy open rooms on the ground and first floors: the library, the diplomatic reception room, the East Room, the Green Room, that stuff. The President's Oval Office is on the other side of the mansion, in the West Wing, overlooking the Rose Garden. No tourists.

There was the predictable line of tourists winding all the way around the block and disappearing behind the tree-shaded curve of South Executive Avenue. I could see them from my office window. Somehow, even this early in the day, they looked worn and bedraggled, kids whining, heat making their tempers short. They looked like a line of refugees whose only sacred possessions were cameras and souvenir balloons.

I took the underground slideway to the White House. It saved time and aggravation. There was a uniformed Marine Corps guard at the basement entrance to the slideway in my building; a half-dozen or more of them in pillboxes along the cleanly tiled tunnel, armed with automatic rifles and God knows what else; and another squad at the end under the White House. When the elevator opened in the West Wing's corridor, a trio of Secret Service agents, all in civvies and very polite, walked me under the identification arch.

The arch is like the old-fashioned inspection machines they have at airports, where they check you and anything you're carrying for weapons. But at the White House, the advanced technology of the identification arch checks your fingerprints, retinal patterns, voice-print, physiognomy, and weight, all in the three seconds it takes you to walk through the portal. All you have to do is say your name aloud and hold your hands up, palms outward, as you walk through. The machinery in the arch checks you out against a preprogrammed list of cleared personnel. If you don't check out, those polite and soft-talking Secret Service men will quietly ask you to wait while they check further on you. If you try to push past them, chances are you'll be dead in less than a minute.

Nobody gets to be President without inspiring a personal loyalty in the people around him. How else do you explain such an unlikely duo as the worldly, urbane Dean Acheson and the bantam rooster from Independence? Or the men around Nixon, who would've rather had their fingernails pulled out than admit anything that would hurt their Chief? Or Morton Rochester, the assistant speechwriter who threw himself on top of a grenade to protect the life of *his* President?

James J. Halliday was my President. God knows I had a tangled web of motivations in my head when I first went to work for him. I still haven't straightened them all out; in fact, now it all seems even more complex and involved. But from the instant I first met him, I felt—hell, I *knew*—that this was a man I'd be proud to work for. In fact, he always gave you the impression you were working with him, not for him. Harrison and the other guys in Boston thought I was stark crazy when I dumped my job there to go to work for Halliday. He was just a "dumb blond" governor from a sparsely populated Western state making a dark horse bid for the Presidential nomination on the strength of his father's money and his handsome face and not much else. They thought.

I had never regretted a moment of that campaign, nor the first few months of his Administration. Halliday showed me more brains, more guts, more honesty than I had ever believed possible in a politician. He was no dummy. He could be ruthless and ice-cold when he wanted to be. He sidestepped traps laid for him by the top people in his own party. He destroyed a few self-styled enemies and then allowed the rest to join him as allies. He cowed them all into working hard and playing it straight.

And, above all, he awed them with his intelligence. There wasn't a facet of the campaign that he didn't know in microscopic detail. From the campaign financing to the intricacies of international economic policies, from dickering with the big unions to negotiating oil treaties with the Saudis, from showing the multinational corporations that a Democrat in the White House would be good for business (and making them believe it) to balancing the Russian Premier and the Chinese Chairman against each other—Halliday displayed the knowledge, the energy, the skills of the previous seven Presidents all wrapped up in one man.

There could be only one man in the world like him, and if someone had planted a double behind his desk in the Oval Office, I would know it immediately. I had seen Halliday through all his moods, all his private agonies, all his public triumphs for more than two years. If the man behind that desk wasn't Halliday, I'd know it.

But, I asked myself as the final security guard opened the office door before me, *what will you do about it?*

Wyatt was in the office, sitting in his usual rocker by the fireplace, under the Remington painting. Lester Lazar, the Vice-President, was in the caneback chair right in front of the desk. He looked like a kindly old country doctor, graying and slightly portly. Actually, he was a New York lawyer who had pulled himself up by his own bootstraps from a poor man's tax adviser in Queens to a big union lawyer on Wall Street.

"Ah, Meric, you're here," said the Vice-President. "You tell him; maybe to you he'll listen."

I walked across to the Scandinavian slingback that I usually sat in during my infrequent visits. As I reached for it, I noticed The Man smiling at me.

"Do you realize you always walk *around* the Great Seal?" he said to me. "You never step on it."

I eased myself into the slingback chair and glanced at the golden eagle with the arrows and olive branch inside a circle of fifty stars; the background of the carpet was blue.

Before I could think of something to get me off the hook, Lazar said, "Was the President's appearance in Boston a success or not, from the public relations point of view?"

The President was smiling easily at me, but Wyatt, tucked away behind Lazar's back, made a sharp "no-

no" motion with his head. The Vice-President wasn't in on the dead duplicate. Which wasn't unusual. Vice-Presidents are seldom privy to the real goings on of the White House.

"It was a smash hit," I said. "I wish I could talk the President into making more public appearances. They loved him."

Lazar flourished a hand in the air. "You see? It's *you* who should go to Detroit, not me. Nobody wants to see the Vice-President . . ."

The Man shook his head, still smiling. "Lester, I'm not going to Detroit. I'm not going to address their meeting . . ."

"Whose meeting?" I blurted.

"The Neo-Luddites," said the Vice-President. "They're putting together a national meeting in Detroit to plan a march on Washington."

"To protest job losses from automation," the President said. Then, turning back to Lazar, "Lester, they know my position. I've made it abundantly clear. We can't slow down the economy by stopping automation. It's the increased productivity from automation that's put the lid on inflation."

"Such as it is."

"Such as it is," the President admitted. "But I will not go to Detroit or anywhere else and promise unemployed workers that I'll put the brakes on automation. And that's what they'd expect to hear."

Lazar raised his eyes to the ceiling.

"In the long run," the President continued, "automation will increase everyone's standard of living."

"And in the short run," Lazar countered, "people are losing jobs to machines, and hating it a lot. A *lot*."

"We've got aid programs . . ."

"They want jobs! And, Mr. President, they want to see you. You're the man they voted for last year; I'm just an afterthought."

The President shook his head.

I had been prodding the President to get out into the

open and meet the people more. He had won the election by campaigning with enormous vigor; he literally outran the opposition. But once he settled into the White House, he had dug in like a cave-dwelling hermit. It was primarily my urging that shook him loose for the Boston trip. He'd originally wanted to address the Faneuil Hall meeting over closed-circuit television.

But the aftermath of the Boston speech was still shaking my guts. I wasn't going to side with Lazar now.

"The people want to see you," Lazar repeated, more weakly.

"Not just now," the President said. "Detroit is the wrong place, and the Neo-Luddites are the wrong crowd."

"You'll be perfectly safe . . ."

"It's not security I'm worrying about." Halliday looked over to Wyatt, then returned his attention to the Vice-President. "Lester, I can't *make* you go to Detroit. But I am asking you to do it."

Lazar made a very Semitic shrug. "Of course I'll do what you ask. But I think you're missing an opportunity to show the people . . ."

"Some other time. Not now."

"All right," Lazar said. "And what should I tell these jobless people?"

The President didn't hesitate an instant. He ticked off on his fingers:

"First, automation is a fact of life. If we tried to stop the automated factories now in operation, our GNP would drop by at least ten percent.

"Second, that means a similar loss of jobs. Unemployment would go up even more, because of the echo effect. There would be *more* people unemployed, not fewer.

"Third, automation means higher productivity, which in turn means lower inflation levels. The prices of consumer goods and food have been holding steady the past few months. Stop automation and . . ."

Lazar held up both his hands in a gesture of surrender. "I know. I know. It's our standard line of reasoning." He let his hands drop and looked wistfully at the President. "But you know, sometimes people don't think with their heads. The opposition, now, they're making a big emotional scene out of this."

"Let them," the President said. "By the end of the year prices will have stabilized and employment should be starting up again. Let them damn the machines then."

The Vice-President stayed and chatted for a few minutes longer, mostly about the local politicians he should butter up in Detroit. And the union people, of course. He was smiling when he left the office. Smiling, but his eyes were still unhappy.

As the door closed behind him, Halliday said to me, "I can only give you a few minutes, Meric. Arguing with the Vice-President always seems to take more time than it's worth."

He was grinning when he said it. Earlier this morning, during our picture-phone review of the day's news, he had seemed tense, impatient, almost angry. Now he was relaxed and friendly. Maybe talking with Lazar did bother him.

"And you've got the Secretary of State due in another fifteen minutes," Wyatt reminded him.

The grin faded only slightly. "Oh, yes, Reynolds's plan for restructuring the Department."

"That's about like trying to restructure mud," His Holiness groused from the rocker.

The President gave a "what the hell" kind of shrug and then turned to me. "McMurtrie tells me you did a fine job last night. I appreciate it."

It all came back into focus immediately. I'd actually been trying to forget the whole thing.

"Do you think we can really keep the press from finding out about it?" he asked.

"For a time," I said. "Nobody can keep them at bay indefinitely."

His face was completely serious now. "I don't like to

skulk around under a cloak of secrecy. There hasn't been a President yet who didn't stub his toes that way."

"This thing is too big and too scary to let loose on the public," His Holiness said.

"You're probably right, Robert," the President answered. "Still . . ." His voice trailed off and he leaned back in his chair, staring at the ceiling the way he always does when he's mulling over a problem. Damn! He looked like Halliday. He sounded like Halliday. He acted like Halliday. But yet . . .

"Mr. President," I asked, and he gave me a cocked eyebrow for being so formal, "what's being done about the situation? I mean, what steps have you taken?"

Halliday glanced at Wyatt, then sat up straight and focused his gaze on me. "McMurtrie is picking a handful of ultrareliable people to serve as an investigating staff. He'll report directly to Robert, here."

"And?"

"And we'll find out what's going on."

I thought I had missed something. "Wait a minute. How does the FBI fit into this? And the National Intelligence Commission? What about . . ."

"We're keeping the investigation small and quiet," the President said.

Wyatt added, "And restricted to people who are personally loyal to the President."

"But . . ."

"The FBI's too damned independent," Wyatt went on. "Always has been. Leaks to the press. Too damned busy keeping its public image polished to maintain the kind of secrecy this needs."

"You do understand," Halliday said to me, "that if any word of this leaks out to the public, we're in for it."

I nodded. "It'd cause a panic, all right."

"Worse than that. If there's the slightest doubt that I am actually the duly-elected President, how do you think the Congress will react? What do you think will happen to every piece of legislation we've sent over to the Hill?"

"There'll be a hundred and fifty investigating committees formed overnight," Wyatt growled.

"Maybe that's not such a bad idea," I heard myself say. And immediately wished I hadn't.

Anyone else would have at least frowned. I could see Wyatt, out of the corner of my eye, scowl darkly at me. But The Man grinned.

"Why do you say that, Meric?" he asked.

I was stuck with it. "We-ell . . . if there's a lot of noise and hoopla about the incident, then whoever's trying to slip a double in here might get scared off."

The President looked over to Wyatt. "Hadn't thought about that angle of it. Have you?"

"It's not worth thinking about," he answered testily. "The whole goddamned Government would grind to a halt while everybody in the world tried to figure out if you are who you claim you are."

"I suppose so," Halliday said.

"This isn't the first time?" I asked. "It's happened before?"

He nodded. "In Denver, just before the Inauguration. A body was found in the same hotel Laura and I were in, the night before we left for Washington."

"He looked just like you?"

"So they tell me. I didn't see him. McMurtrie had been assigned to me all through the campaign. He took care of it. Cleaning woman discovered the body, I understand, and ran into one of McMurtrie's men without even taking a look at the corpse's face."

"Lucky," I said.

Wyatt grumbled, "With a little more luck like that we can all go down the chute."

I must have been staring at the President, because he gave me his slow, personal smile and said, "It's okay, Meric. It's really me."

I shook my head. "I'm sorry. It's just that . . . I, hell, I'm scared of this."

"That's a healthy reaction."

"But don't you think you ought to be digging into this harder? Deeper? I mean, McMurtrie's a body-guard, not a detective. You've got the entire apparatus of the Government at your disposal . . ."

He stopped me with an upraised hand. "Meric . . . Meric. Think a minute. I'm not Premier Blagdanoff, much less Chairman Chao. It's not *my* Government. I don't own it, and I can't use it to suit my whim."

"But the intelligence people . . . the Justice Department . . ."

"Might be in on it," Wyatt snapped.

"What?"

"How do we know who we can trust? Somebody's doing this . . . somebody damned close to the White House. Maybe somebody *in* the White House." The blue vein in the old man's forehead throbbed angrily.

Halliday fixed him with a gaze. "Robert, this is no time to go paranoid."

"I know, I know . . ."

"That's another reason why this investigation must be kept as small and quiet as possible. We could unleash a witch hunt that would make the McCarthy craze in the fifties and Alonzo's purge of the eighties look like kindergarten games. We've got to keep things under control." And his hands pressed flat on the desk top, a gesture I had seen him use in moments of stress a hundred times.

"But McMurtrie can't handle it," I insisted. "He isn't the right man for the job."

It was my turn to get stared at. "He's the man I assigned to handle it," the President said. His voice was calm, quiet, and iron hard.

I guess I still didn't look convinced, because he went on, "He'll have access to anyone in the Executive branch of Government that he wants. He can pick out the best team of investigators that the nation can produce. But it will be a small team, working directly for McMurtrie, on leave from the regular departments."

"And reporting to me," Wyatt said, "instead of some

agency director who's worried more about his bureaucracy than the life of the President."

I said nothing. Their minds were made up.

"There are three possibilities," the President said, hunching forward in his chair and ticking off the points on his fingers.

"First, it might be a foreign plan to get rid of me and install an agent in my place. That sounds pretty wild to me. It just isn't the way governments think or work."

"That doesn't mean it can't be real," Wyatt said.

Halliday shrugged lightly and went on. "Second, it might be a group inside the Government here, say, the military, who want to get me out and their own man in."

I said, "The Joint Chiefs don't think too much of the way you're handling this Kuwait trouble."

"I realize that. But it's hard to think that nearly two and a quarter centuries of civilian control over the military is being threatened by the Joint Chiefs."

"You really think they're that loyal to you?"

"To the nation, yes. Unqualifiedly. And I haven't really frightened them to the point where they think they've got to take over the Presidency to save the nation."

Wyatt shook his head. "It only takes a couple of paranoids."

"No," the President insisted. "It takes a lot more than that to make exact duplicates and get them as close to me as the two dead bodies have gotten."

"What killed them?" I wondered aloud.

The President ignored that and went on to his third point. "Finally, there's the chance that some interest group within the United States, but not inside the Government, is behind it. Same reason: they want to get their own man into the White House."

"Who could it be?" I asked.

Wyatt shouted. "Anybody! This Administration's been straightening out a lot of overdue problems. And everytime we try to help one group, at least one other group gets sore because they think we're hurting them.

I could give you a list as long as this room: every goddamned pressure group from the National Association of Cattlemen to the Boy Scouts."

"It's not that bad," the President murmured.

"No? The auto manufacturers are sore because we've pushed them into upping pensions for the workers retired early by automation. The unions are sore because we're backing automation and robots are taking more new jobs than people. The farmers. The truckers. Those damned fat cats on Wall Street. The blacks in the cities who're madder'n hell at being forced to work for their welfare checks . . ." He ran out of breath.

"You can't change society without frightening people," the President said. "Even those who yell the loudest for change are frightened when it comes."

"And what they're scared of, they hate."

"And what they hate," I finished, "they strike out against."

"Exactly," said the President.

"So you think it's the third alternative? Some power group outside the Government?"

"Yes. That's my hunch."

"Some damned well-heeled pressure group," Wyatt said. "This is no gaggle of ghetto kids making bombs in their lofts. It's the big leaguers."

"But . . ." Something about that conclusion just didn't hit me right. "But they have all sorts of other avenues to fight you. They've got Congressmen and Senators in their pockets. Money. Influence. The media. Why *this?*"

Halliday leaned back in his chair again. "I've been asking myself the same question, Meric. And there's only one possible answer. Some group in the United States has decided that the democratic process doesn't work the way they want it to. They're not content to let the people decide. They want to take over the Government. Of themselves. By themselves. For themselves."

For a few long moments I sat there saying nothing. The room was absolutely quiet. Sunlight streamed in through the ceiling-high windows. Outside, the rose garden was a picture of tranquillity. I imagined I could hear bees droning as they went from bloom to bloom.

Then I looked at Halliday. The President was watching me, appraising my reactions.

"It scares the shit out of me," I said.

"I know. Me too."

"You really ought to be doing more than sending McMurtrie out to round up a team of investigators. A lot more."

"Like what?" His Holiness snapped. "Call out the Marines? Declare a national emergency?"

It was so damned *frustrating*. "If I knew, I'd tell you."

"I don't think there's much more we can do, at this stage," the President said softly.

"You can dig into those goddamned pressure groups," Wyatt demanded. *"Use* the FBI. And Internal Revenue. Stir up their nests! Force them into a wrong move. Take the initiative."

He cocked his head slightly to one side, the way he always does when he wants to give the impression he's seriously considering something. But almost immediately he answered, "And we'll be taking another step toward a police state. Those pressure groups are people, Robert. Most of them haven't done anything at all that's even vaguely illegal. We can't go bursting in on them like a gang of storm troopers. That would do more harm than good."

Wyatt groused and pitched back and forth impatiently on the rocker. "All right. *Most* of those people are good citizens, although I'll bet you can find a lot of dirt under their fingernails. But *some* of them are trying to kill you."

There it was. Out in the open.

Halliday said simply, "Then we'd better find out which ones they are before they succeed, hadn't we?"

CHAPTER FOUR

I had lunch with Wyatt in the tiny staff dining room in the West Wing. We talked over the possible problems of handling the press and the media, should any of this business leak out.

Calling it a dining room was being overgenerous. It was a glorified cafeteria, down in the basement under the West Wing, barely big enough to hold a dozen people at one time. Completely automated food service, like coin machines except that these were free. Your tax dollars at work. Dead-white walls with no decorations outside of a TV screen that served as a bulletin board, constantly flashing news items, press releases, job descriptions, and other tidbits that no one paid any attention to. The furniture was a bit posh for a cafeteria: slim-legged teak tables and rope-weave chairs. Very comfortable. The only other people in the little room were a pair of security guards, both female, chatting about their coming evening. Wyatt and I sat as far from them as we could.

In between bites of a sandwich that tasted like plastic on cardboard, I said, "Robert, there's one absolutely essential point. I can't cover for you if I don't know what's happening."

He gave me a hawkish look from across the narrow teak table. "Afraid of being caught in public with your pants down?"

"I can stand the embarrassment," I countered evenly, "but you can't. And neither can the President. Once those news people get the impression that I'm not

45

giving them the straight story, they'll swarm all over us. We can't afford that."

And a corner of my mind was saying, *How easily you switch from being open, honest, and a responsible civil servant to being secretive, misleading, and plotting to keep the truth away from the people.*

Wyatt chewed on his salad thoughtfully for a few moments, then said, "Okay, we'll keep you fully informed."

"How?"

He almost smiled at me. "You're learning, Meric. A few days ago and you would've accepted my word on it and not worried about how the agreement would be implemented."

"A few days ago I was young and innocent."

"And now?"

"Now I'm scared. Somebody's trying to steal this whole damned country from us, Robert!"

He did smile this time. "Don't get panicky. That won't help."

"But how can you stay so calm?"

His smile faded and his mouth went tight and hard. His eyes, the cold blue of polar ice, bored into me. "Because," he whispered harshly, "we're going to find whoever it is who's trying to assassinate the President. They are not going to succeed. We are going to find them and crush them."

And his frail, liver-spotted hands snapped the plastic fork he was holding. The pieces fell silently into his salad.

He seemed embarrassed. "Excuse me." He got to his feet and brushed at his slacks. "It's time I got back to my office."

I got up and reached across the table to grasp his arm. "Robert. You didn't answer my question."

"Eh? Oh . . . you've got a direct wire to me. Use it. I'll keep you up-to-the-minute."

"Not good enough," I said.

He pulled his arm loose and glared at me as I came around the table to stand in front of him. I'm not a very big guy, but I felt as if I were looming over him. He was so old and frail-looking.

But made of steel. "Just what is it you want, Meric? Do I have to buy you off?"

"Right on. I want to have full access to McMurtrie. If he's heading this investigation, I want to be able to talk directly to him, go where he goes, know what he knows."

"That's ridiculous."

"That's my price," I said, knowing that McMurtrie was not only doggedly loyal but as thoroughly honest as any man I'd ever met. If Wyatt told him he could answer any questions I asked, I'd be kept fully informed, and we both knew it.

Wyatt's eyes narrowed. "You don't have any ideas of playing detective yourself, do you? All you newsmen . . ."

"Robert, all I want is to be kept informed. Honestly and completely."

He hesitated just a moment longer. Then, "I'll speak to McMurtrie about it."

"Good."

"He won't like it, you realize."

"He doesn't have to."

Wyatt nodded once, just an abrupt snap of his head, and then turned and strode out of the dining room. I stood there and watched him. *He should wear a sword,* I thought. *He's got that kind of regal bearing.*

Just as I was heading out the door myself, the PA microphone in the tiled ceiling called in a soft female voice, "Mr. Albano, please dial four-six-six. Mr. Albano . . ."

The wall phone was right beside the doors: an old no-picture, voice-only model. I picked up the receiver and punched the buttons.

"Meric Albano here."

"One moment, please, sir." The same operator's voice. There was a hesitation just long enough for a computer to scan my voiceprint. Then, "Meric? Is that you?"

The floor dropped away from under me. "Yes, it's me, Laura."

"How are you?" Her voice told me that she didn't really care, one way or the other.

"What do you want?" I realized I was whispering into the phone's mouthpiece. *Like a goddamned kid snitching a date behind his best friend's back.*

"I have to talk to you."

"Sure."

"Today. This afternoon."

"You know where my office . . ." That was ridiculous. The First Lady doesn't drop in on the hired help. Especially the ones she used to live with. "I'm in the West Wing right now. I can come up and . . ."

"No, not here," she said. "I'm going shopping this afternoon. At the new Beltway Plaza."

"Why not make it the Lincoln Memorial? It'll be less crowded."

She ignored my dripping satire. "Can you meet me at Woodies there? Four-thirty?"

"It's a big place."

"At the front entrance. I *have to* talk with you."

Like a patient who's just decided to risk his second heart transplant, I said, "I'll be there."

"Thank you, Meric."

Before I could say anything else she clicked off.

It was a swell afternoon. I growled at Greta when I got back to the office, slammed my door shut, and sat at my desk, staring out the window, trying to make the time go faster by sheer mental will power. Didn't work. After sweating it out for an hour, I glanced at my desk clock; barely five minutes had passed.

So I tried to work. I shuffled papers and answered a few phone calls. I didn't make much sense, not even to myself. I told Greta to cancel the rest of the day's appointments. She gave me her "you need some chicken soup" look, but went ahead and broke several hearts for me.

Around three, somebody tapped on the door and

came right in. I was staring out the window again, and swung around in my chair, starting to growl, "I gave specific instru—"

It was Vickie, looking troubled. Immediately I felt like a louse. She had such a sunny face, normally. Hair the color of California gold, thick and short cropped.

"What is it?" I asked, trying to make it sound reasonably polite.

She stood in the middle of the room, halfway between the chairs in front of the desk and the couch along the side wall.

"The planning session for next week's meeting of the National Association of News Media Managers," Vickie said, a bit hesitantly. "Greta said you won't be able to get together with us this afternoon. Should we cancel the session or . . ."

"Oh, shit. I've got to give that speech in St. Louis next week, don't I?"

She came as far as the chair, looking a little like a wary faun. "You don't want to let much more time go by without working out your speech. I've got all the background material for it, but . . ."

"Yeah, I know. You're right." I felt a headache coming on and rubbed at my forehead.

"Are you okay?" Vickie asked.

"Yeah, fine . . . super."

"What happened last night?"

I took a good look at her. She was concerned; it was written on her face. But she wasn't frightened or shaken the way I was. She didn't know anything more than I was showing her. Or did she?

"What do you mean?"

Vickie leaned slightly on the back of the chair. "We sat in the plane for more than two hours, waiting for you and McMurtrie. You were the last one aboard, and then the two of you huddled together like a couple of high school girls discussing your dates."

She probably used that metaphor to make me smile. I frowned.

"Listen," I said. "There are times when it's our job

to prevent stories from being written. Especially when the stories are nothing more than trumped-up rumors. That's what I was doing last night."

"Oh? What hap—"

"Nothing happened," I snapped. "Nothing that I want to talk about. Nothing that I want *you* to talk about. To anyone. Understand?"

Her perky little nose wrinkled. "Is that an order, boss?"

"Damned right. And I know it violates the First Amendment, so don't go judicial on me. Just forget that anything unusual happened last night."

She didn't like it at all, but she said, "If you say so."

As Vickie left the office, I wondered how long she'd sit still about this. She was a bright and aggressive kid. No reporter, she was a researcher. She delighted in digging into things and pulling out hidden facts. And how many others were in that staff plane wondering about the same thing?

The Beltway Plaza is a city within the city. Once the Beltway was a circumferential highway, well out in the woods, built with the idea of helping Interstate highway motorists—and truckers—get past Washington without getting entangled in city traffic.

It immediately became a circumferential focus for new housing developments, office complexes, light industry, shopping malls, helicopter pads, truckers' restaurants, hotels, whorehouses, banks—all the conveniences and congestions of urban living. The Beltway itself still existed; it was even a double-decked roadway now. But it was almost always jammed with everything from heavy semis delivering the daily bread to little electric hatchbacks driven by young mothers out for their shopping, hairdressing, or what-have-you.

By 4:15 I was pacing in front of the main entrance to the Woodward & Lothrop department store at the Beltway Plaza. The shopping mall was built on the highest point of the complex, a small hill, but high enough so that the aluminum and glass of the mall dominated the walled-in apartment buildings, swimming pools, school, and hotel of the Plaza community. It was like a palace in the center of a walled city. The community was walled in with electric fences and laser intruder alarms to protect the inhabitants from the barbarians of the old, decayed areas of Greater Washington. Protect them not only from attack, but from the sight of scrawny, scruffy ghetto dwellers. Out of sight, out of mind. Except for the welfare tax bills, which got bigger every year. And the occasional violence that was usually, but not always, confined to the ghettos.

This was one of the major problems that the Halliday Administration had attacked. And one of the reasons why the President insisted on increasing productivity as a means of stabilizing inflation. With a typical Halliday combination of compassion and ruthlessness, he knew that the economy had to keep growing in order to bring prosperity to the poor. "Turn the welfare recipients into taxpayers," he told us. It wasn't easy.

The Man was battling the objections of the unions and starting urban rebuilding projects within the city ghettos, using strictly local labor. The projects were actually combinations of training programs and pride-builders. They also sapped the power of the unions, something that Halliday openly deplored because the unions were wrong to ignore the needs of the minority ethnic groups, not because it made them less effective politically.

Anyone—man, woman, or child—caught burglarizing, mugging, or otherwise trying to redress the difference between rich and poor through violence was shipped off to construction camps in the Far West. The Man's opponents howled that this was unconstitutional and the camps were nothing more than concentration camps. Halliday produced a long string of ecologists and psychiatrists to show that: (a) the camp internees were making positive inroads in correcting the environmental damages done by earlier strip mining, river pollution, and other ravages of the land; and (b) the internees were adjusting to this useful outdoor life, gaining some sense of responsibility and self-esteem, and saving much of the cash they were paid for their work.

Halliday's long-term plan was to build new communities in the land the internees had reclaimed and let them settle there permanently. He insisted that returning a ghetto kid to the place where he had committed his crime was merely inviting him to commit more crimes. The psychologists were behind him on this, but a strange combination of urban political bosses, real estate manipulators, and civil libertarians had formed a coalition against the program.

They preferred to sit in their armed, walled-in enclaves and let the cities crumble. I paced back and forth across the department store's main entrance, watching the shoppers hustle in and out, their faces intent on buying and prices and what to do about dinner tonight. They weren't thinking ahead. They seldom did.

My mind had wandered so far afield that I nearly jumped out of my boots when someone tapped me on the shoulder.

I turned to see a Secret Service security guard type, neatly dressed in a conservative suit that was probably bulging with armaments.

"The First Lady will see you on the roof of the store, sir," he said quietly, automatically eyeing the shoppers passing by us, "near the helicopter pad."

He quietly led me through the store. It wasn't very crowded. Most of the Plaza housewives were on their way home now to prepare dinners for their husbands and kids. I wondered why the management maintained such a big, expensive store when anyone with a modern picture-phone and home computer could do all the shopping from bed. But then I guessed that the store was more of a showplace, a central meeting ground, an entertainment center, an excuse to get out of the house.

All this philosophizing, of course, was my feeble way of keeping me from getting all worked up about seeing Laura. Think about other things—an old Catholic remedy. But as I rode up three flights of escalators behind that Secret Service guard, I could feel my temperature rising. We went through an office area and up a flight of metal stairs, my pulse throbbing in my ears louder and louder with each step.

He opened a metal door and we stepped out onto the cement roof. A blue and white helicopter sat in the middle of the flat expanse, idle and empty. Smallish job; probably could hold no more than six. The rest of the roof was bare, unoccupied.

"Mrs. Halliday will be here in a few minutes," the security man said. He shut the metal door, leaving me totally alone on the roof.

A decent breeze was blowing, and from up here I could see all the way across the sprawling rooftops of Greater Washington to the Monument's spire sticking into the light blue springtime sky. Some high wispy cirrus were the only clouds, except for the contrails of jets.

I walked over to the edge of the roof, feeling like a duke standing atop a king's palace, surveying his liege's domain, about to have a private meeting with his queen. *Dangerous business,* I thought. *Especially if the king doesn't know about it.*

It suddenly hit me that I was very vulnerable. Physically. Alone up here on the roof, I made an easy target for a sniper perched on any of the other rooftops around this building. I backed away from the edge. The *thwap-thwap-thwap* of a nearby helicopter startled me. They could get me from the air.

I could feel myself sinking into paranoid fears when the metal door opened again and three security men stepped through. I stood frozen, as if my shoes had been welded to the rooftop's concrete. But they ignored me totally and fanned out across the roof to take up stations exactly 120 degrees apart. You didn't need any measuring instruments to know how precise these guys were.

A half-minute passed; then the door opened again and Laura came through, followed immediately by two more guards. One stayed at the door and the other walked straight past me to the helicopter.

Laura came to where I stood, still rooted—but for another reason now. She smiled and held out her hand.

"Hello, Meric. It was good of you to come."

This was the first time I'd seen her, close enough to talk to, to touch, since the Inauguration. And the first time I'd seen her without Halliday between us in nearly three years. She was stunning. You've seen her face on all the magazine covers and on television. You've heard beauty experts take her apart, claiming her eyes are a bit too large for the shape of her face, her cheekbones a shade too prominent, her lips thinner than they ought to be. Fuck 'em all. She was beautiful.

She gave the impression of being tall, although actually she was a head shorter than I am. (She looked taller with Halliday, for some reason.) Dark, dark hair, pulled straight back. And a slightly olive cast to her complexion that hinted of Mediterranean origins. The slim, almost boyish body of a ballet dancer. The first time we had made love, my first sight of her naked body had almost dismayed me, she looked so bony and stringy. But I quickly learned that she was soft enough. And wondrously supple.

It was awful. I felt like a kid who'd been caught jerking off in the bathroom. My throat was dry, my palms sweaty.

"Hello, Laura," I managed to say. My voice sounded cracked and hoarse.

"You've put on a little weight," she teased. "Washington life agrees with you."

"Rubber chicken . . . the banquet circuit."

She nodded and toyed with the shoulder strap of her handbag. She was wearing a sleeveless white dress, very summery. No sunglasses. Her eyes were just as gray-green as ever.

"You wanted to talk to me," I said.

She took a deliberate slow breath, like an athlete preparing herself for a supreme effort.

"Yes," Laura said. "I know about what happened last night. And in Denver."

"And?"

"And I know Jim has asked you to keep the entire matter hushed up."

"We talked about it this morning, he and Wyatt and I."

"Yes." She looked up at me, searching my face. It was all I could do to keep my hands at my sides. "Meric ... I've got to know where you stand on this. You might ... well, it occurred to me that you might not *want* to keep the story quiet."

I guess I blinked at her. "Why?"

She suddenly looked annoyed. "It's a story that could ruin Jim. And you ... the two of us ... before I met him ..."

"Hold it," I said. "You're afraid that I'll blow the story open to hurt him? Or you?"

"I know it's wrong for me even to suggest it ..."

"It sure as hell is!" I snapped. "Okay, so I'm still zonked-out over you. But what kind of a son of a bitch do you think I am? I *work* for The Man. I work *for* him."

"I know, I know ... it was stupid of me to ask. But I couldn't help wondering ... I had to hear it from you ..."

"You never did understand me," I grumbled. "You want me to swear a loyalty oath? You want to go down to a bookstore and find a stack of Bibles?"

"Don't, Meric. That's not fair."

"The hell it isn't! You had to hear it from me in person. Crap! Sounds like something His Holiness would do—him and his suspicious goddamned mind."

Her expression changed. "I did speak with Robert about you . . ." She let her voice trail off.

"He put you up to this?"

She looked away from me. "I wouldn't say it that way. But . . . well, I did begin to wonder . . . about you . . . about how you'd react . . . after he spoke to me."

"That gritty old bastard," I fumed.

She put her hand on my arm and started making soothing sounds and offered me a ride back downtown in her chopper. I went along with her, probably wagging my tail like a puppy dog that'd just gotten a pat on its head from its mistress.

It wasn't until I was safely back in my apartment, and the city outside had gone dark with night, that I realized Wyatt couldn't possibly have talked with her before she called me. He and I had been together in the West Wing staff dining room when she had called.

CHAPTER FIVE

St. Louis is a dull town. The people are dull. The atmosphere is humid and oppressive. Old Man River is wide and sluggish and closed in on both banks by factories that keep the water rank and brown, despite a whole generation's steady work at cleaning up the pollution. The factory owners buy off the city fathers, who not only pocket the graft, but get extra money from Washington for pollution control, since they can show that their pollution problems are still serious. It was something that Halliday had his personal hounds sniffing at; the smell was easy to detect, but tracking it back to its source—with courtroom-tight proof—was another matter.

The hotel where I stayed was dull, too. The staff was downright sullen, as if they resented the idea of cash customers who asked them to rouse themselves and put out a little work. I got the feeling that the chambermaids would be perfectly happy to let me make my own bed. The bartender down in the lobby was no better. Even the lifeguard at the fenced-in pool acted as if his duty were to prevent anybody from disturbing the water. The pool was nearly deserted.

The National Association of News Media Managers held their meeting in the hotel's main ballroom, which was beautifully decorated in Gay Nineties gilt and rococo: cherubs on the ceiling, bunches of gilded grapes adorning the window frames, heavy velvet drapes. I half-expected to see Mark Twain give the first evening's keynote address, instead of me. He would have done a lot better.

They applauded my speech, all fifteen hundred of the NANMM representatives, especially the trigger words Vickie and my staff had put in: *freedom of information, open access to the newsmakers, making the Constitution work,* and *the healthy adversary relationship between the Government and the news media.* Especially that last one; they loved that one.

These overweight desk jockeys, these owners of newspapers and television stations, these white-haired tight-fisted executives who had never been on the firing line trying to dig the truth out of a reluctant politician, who had suppressed more stories about their friends than they ever published about their enemies—these money handlers loved to think they were Hildy Johnson, Ed Murrow, Walter Lippmann, and Horace Greeley, all rolled into one. They pictured themselves as Citizen Kane, and maybe in that, at least, they were close to the mark.

So I gave them what they wanted to hear, and they applauded enthusiastically. Up until the previous week, I would have believed what I was telling them. The Halliday Administration *was* open, honest, and anxious to play fair with the press—not these stuffed penguins and their bejeweled ladies, but the real, working press.

But while I was speaking those glowing platitudes to them, I knew that I was sitting on the biggest story of them all, and I wasn't going to tell anyone about it.

I made polite conversation through the reception after my speech, and got back to my suite upstairs as fast as I could. I felt drained, exhausted. And—as there had been for the past week—somewhere deep inside of me there was a fear gnawing away, like that last instant of a nightmare just before you awake, falling, falling, falling into something dark and terrible.

It was after midnight. My hotel suite was plush: bed big enough for half a dozen people, automated bar, comfortable sitting room for entertaining business guests. I plopped on the bed and called Vickie's home number. The phone buzzed four times. I was about to click off when her voice answered, throaty and sleepy. The screen stayed a flickering gray. Then I realized it was after 1:00 A.M. in Washington.

"I woke you up," I said. "I'm sorry."

"Meric?" Her voice brightened. "Hi. I must've just dozed off. I was sort of expecting you to call. Wait half a minute . . ."

The screen cleared and showed her, yellow hair tousled and eyes a little bleary. She had a green robe pulled up around her throat.

"How'd the speech go?" she asked.

"Good enough."

"Count the applause?"

"No, let the computer analyze it when the tapes get to the office tomorrow."

"You're down."

"It's a down city," I said.

But she was looking at me from the phone screen very intently. "No, you've been down for the past week or more. Whatever it is, it's really got you bugged."

"Never mind. I'll live through it."

"It started when she called you, didn't it?"

"She?"

"The First Lady." Somehow Vicki put an accent on the word "lady" that wasn't entirely wholesome.

"Laura's got nothing to do with it," I said.

Vickie just shook her head. She wasn't buying a word of it.

We just sat there for a silent moment or two, neither of us wanting to say anything, neither of us wanting to break the connection. I was totally alone except for this flickering electronic image of her.

"The convention's not much fun?" Vickie asked at last.

"Bunch of bloodsuckers," I grumbled. "I'm surrounded by the kinds of people I had to fight when I was a reporter. Fight them for raises. Fight to get the *real* news printed, the stuff they wanted to cover up to protect their friends. Now I'm a big-time political person. I'm supposed to smile at them and tell 'em we're all in this together."

She laughed, and the sound of it made me smile, too. "It's a good thing you didn't go into the State Department."

"Yeah," I admitted, "maybe so."

"Will you be able to stand it for another day? You're scheduled for three network interviews tomorrow."

"That's okay. That's with the working slobs. I get along fine with them."

She tried to stifle a yawn.

"Hunter do okay with the daily briefing this morning?"

"Oh, yes," Vickie said. "He was fine. No problems." She yawned again.

"Aw, hell, I shouldn't be keeping you up all night—"

"I don't mind," she said.

"But I do. Go to bed. We both need some sleep."

"Meric?"

"Yeah?"

"I wish I were there with you." She wasn't smiling when she said it. She said it straight out, no games, no tricks.

Without thinking about it for an instant, I decided to misunderstand her. "You'd be just as bored and sore at this bunch of self-righteous hypocrites as I am."

Her face didn't change expression. But her voice went fainter. "Yes. I guess so."

"Good night, Vickie."

"Good night."

I touched the button on the tiny keyboard alongside the phone, and its screen went blank and dead.

Shit! Added to everything else, now I was sore at myself.

The phone chimed softly. I punched the response button. A woman's face filled the screen: middle-aged, but well kept; expensive makeup and hair styling.

"Mr. Albano, are you retiring for the evening?"

I had seen her before. Where? Behind the hotel

service desk down in the lobby, when I had checked in that morning.

"Yes," I said.

"Is there anything we can provide for you?"

I heard myself chuckle. "Sure. A fifth of Scotch, a bucket of ice, and a tall redhead."

She didn't even blink. "Any particular age?"

"On the Scotch?"

"That, too."

"Make it the best Scotch you've got. And the lady should be in her twenties. I'll settle for that."

"Certainly, sir."

Like the rest of the hotel's services, my nightcap left a lot to be desired. The redhead was willing, even enthusiastic. She was young and well built, the kind that would go to fat in another five years. Big bouncy siliconed breasts. And a brain the size of a walnut. Most intellectual topic of discussion: the local hockey team. Apparently she and another girl were keeping the visiting teams so busy that they inevitably lost when they played in St. Louis. So she claimed. Showed me a purseful of still photos of herself, her friend, and the top stars of the hockey league. Offered to run a video-tape cassette in the room's TV, if I'd add twenty to her fee.

At least she didn't talk with her mouth full.

I got through the interviews the next day with a buzzing head and a rasping conscience. While I was sitting there pontificating on freedom of the press and being congratulated for my forthrightness by the interviewers (Why are they all so alike? Movie idol faces, leather jackets and flowered shirts that were "mod" years ago, fag-English accents) the inside of my head was shouting at me that I was just as big a hypocrite as anybody in the game. The President was in danger and I was playing it quiet.

The last interview that afternoon was conducted by a boy-girl team. It was a typical TV studio: one corner cluttered with the benches and phony ship's deck of a kiddies' show; across the way, the podium, clocks, maps for the evening news show. We were sitting under the lights on a comfortable pile of cushions arranged to look like a conversation pit in a Persian palace. Sure enough, the "boy" half of the interview team wore a rust suede jacket and a gold silk shirt. At least the "girl"—a sharp-eyed woman in her thirties—had the brains to wear a slacks and vest outfit, the kind that lots of women were wearing back on the East Coast.

Halfway through the interview she impatiently interrupted her teammate to ask me, "But what's the President really like? I mean, in person? When the doors are closed and the cameras are off?"

I shifted mental gears and launched into my standard paean of praise about *James J. Halliday, the man.* Sure, we had worked out this spiel in the office, but most of it was from the heart. We didn't have to labor very long or hard to come up with a good three minutes' worth of glowing description about The Man. We all liked him.

But while my mouth was going through its motions, my brain decided that if I liked The Man so goddamned much I shouldn't be sitting on these nonallergenic cushions talking about him. I ought to be helping him to find out who, or what, was trying to kill him.

I put in a call to McMurtrie right there in the studio as soon as the interview was over. It was late afternoon, nearly 4:00 P.M.

The White House operator told me that Mr. McMurtrie was out of town on a special assignment.

"Where?" I asked.

She looked like a chicken. Beady eyes, hooked little nose, pinched pasty-skinned face. She clucked impatiently once and answered, "We are not permitted to reveal that information."

I reminded her of who I was and showed her my ID again. No go. I went over her head, to the Secret Service man in charge of White House security in McMurtrie's absence. He was even stonier. Finally I had to get to Wyatt, and that took damned near half an hour.

His Holiness hemmed and grumbled but finally told me McMurtrie had gone out to some laboratory in Minnesota. Something to do with Dr. Klienerman and the investigation.

"What's the name of the lab?" I asked. "Where in Minnesota?"

It was like trying to break into Fort Knox with a cheese knife, but finally the old man grudgingly told me what I wanted to know. I had to threaten to resign, just about, to get him to open up.

I called Vickie and told her not to expect me in the office the next day; Hunter would have to play "meet the press" for me again. She looked surprised, even startled. Before she could ask why, or where I was going to be, I clicked off and punched the number for airlines information. Thank God it was computerized. No arguing, no explaining, no back talk. Just tell the computer where you are and where you want to go, and the lovely electronic machine gives you a choice of times and routes. I picked a plane that was leaving for Minneapolis in an hour. The computer assured me that my ticket would be waiting at the gate. I rushed off to throw my dirty laundry into my flight bag and head out to the airport.

It was raining by the time I boarded the plane. We sat at the end of the runway for twenty minutes, exposed in the middle of the flat, open airport, engines whining and wind howling and shaking the plane, while the pilot cheerfully explained that a line of squalls and tornadoes was passing over the area. I couldn't see anything outside my little oval window except a solid sheet of rain and an almost constant flickering of lightning. The rain drummed on the plane's fuselage, and the thunder rumbled louder than the engines.

After one really nerve-shattering clap of thunder the pilot told the stewardesses to pass out free drinks. They were just at the row of chairs ahead of mine when he came on the microphone again: "Okay, folks, we just got clearance for take off. Button everything up, ladies."

And through the rain and slackening wind, we took off. The plane was buffeted terribly until we cleared the cloud deck, and then the golden-red late afternoon sun turned the cloudtops into a horizon-spanning carpet of purple velvet. By the time they started serving drinks again I had dozed off.

It was noticeably chillier in Minneapolis when we landed, and I saw that the Twin Cities Airport runways and ramps were wet and puddled. But in the last dying light of the setting sun, I could see that the clouds were hurrying off eastward and the sky was clearing. *Probably get rained on by the same storm again tomorrow, in Washington,* I thought.

Nobody at the rent-a-car booth in the airport had ever heard of the North Lake Research Laboratories, the place that Wyatt had touted me onto. The woman who was making out my car rental forms even phoned the University of Minnesota, and drew a blank there. I knew it was just outside the town of Stillwater, though, so she gave me a map and directions for getting there. Even phoned ahead for a reservation at the Stillwater Inn.

Driving up the Interstate on my way to Stillwater, I had more than an hour to size up my situation.

Point number one: I was acting like a damned fool. Okay, but I was doing what I felt I had to do. Maybe it was the old newshawk instinct. More likely just a combination of fear and curiosity about the unknown. All I knew was that I had to see McMurtrie and Klienerman and find out for myself what in hell was going on.

Point number two: Nobody in the whole world knew where I was. Correction. Robert H. H. Wyatt knew. Or did he? His Holiness knew I was trying to get in touch with McMurtrie. I never told him I was coming up here in person. Didn't even tell Vickie. Wyatt could figure it out soon enough tomorrow, when Hunter called in for the morning press briefing instead of me.

But not until tomorrow morning. No reason for him to miss me tonight.

Which led to point number three: Nobody at the North Lake Research Laboratories knew I was going to drop in on them. I decided to use an old newsman's trick and just show up at their doorstep tomorrow morning, unannounced and unexplained, and demand to see the top man. Hit 'em before they can phony a story together.

I nearly missed the turnoff onto I-94 as I suddenly realized what my mind was doing. I was counting Wyatt, McMurtrie, Klienerman, and whoever runs North Lake Labs as possible suspects. Potential assassins. Traitors plotting to take over the Presidency.

Which brought me to the logical conclusion of all my logical thinking. I realized there was absolutely no one I could trust. Not McMurtrie or Wyatt or Laura or even the President himself. I was totally alone. I couldn't even be sure of Vickie.

I glanced at the bare-branched trees whipping by in the twilight. I felt as if I were alone and naked out there, clinging to one of those dead bare branches. It felt lonely, cold, and damned dangerous.

As the moon came up over the wooded hills, I saw that the highway had now swung along the bank of the mighty Mississippi River. I think they call this part of it the St. Croix, locally. It was a magnificent, wide, beautiful river, cutting through the rolling hills that were dotted with the tiny scatterings of lights that marked little communities and, sometimes, individual homes. The river looked much stronger and somehow younger up here, not like the weary old sick stream that meandered sluggishly past St. Louis. And I knew that a thousand miles southward it finally flowed into the Gulf of Mexico. *It endures. Despite what we do, the river endures. That old songwriter told it truly.*

I found the city of Stillwater at last and, after a couple of wrong turns on its quiet streets, located the Stillwater Inn. It was a lovely, graceful place, kept up as it must have looked in its prime a century ago. As I parked the car in the unattended lot alongside the inn's white clapboard side wall, I started thinking again.

I hadn't pulled any rank at the airports, just used my regular personal charge card to get the airline tickets and the rental card. No fanfare, no Washington connection. But no cover-up, either. Wyatt, or somebody else, could track me down easily enough if he wanted to. But so far, I hadn't called attention to myself.

I checked in at the hotel, paid cash in advance, ate dinner in their Bavarian-styled paneled dining room, had a drink in the coziest little bar I'd ever seen, and then went to my room. Despite all my suspicions and fears, I slept very soundly. I don't even remember dreaming, although I woke up the next morning at dawn's first light, soaked with sweat and very shaky.

CHAPTER SIX

North Lake Research Laboratories was perched on a bluff overlooking the St. Croix, about a half-hour's drive above Stillwater. There were no road signs showing the way, and nobody at the hotel had seemed to know anything about the lab. I had to find the local fire station and ask the old man who was washing down the town's shiny new pumper. Firemen always know what's where, and the quickest way to get there.

From the highway you could see the lab buildings, low and dun gray, hugging the top of the bluff. Midcentury cement and glass architecture, Saarinen by way of Frank Lloyd Wright. My rented car climbed the switch-backed driveway slowly; battery was running down. There was a riotwire fence around the lab enclosure, with a sturdy-looking gate blocking the driveway and a sturdier-looking guard posted in a little phone booth of a sentry box alongside the gate.

I pulled up and he came out, leaned his face down to my window.

"Yessir, what can I do for you?" Very polite. He had an automatic pistol holstered at his hip.

"I'm here to see Mr. McMurtrie and Dr. Klienerman," I said.

The names seemed unfamiliar to him. He looked politely puzzled.

"Dr. Klienerman's from Walter Reed Hospital. Mr. McMurtrie's from the White House."

"Oh . . . yes . . ."

"My name's Albano," I said, before he could ask.

"Meric Albano." I fished out my ID, the one with the Presidential Seal on it.

He started to whistle, impressed, but caught himself. "Just one moment, Mr. Albano. I'll phone the reception lobby."

He did that, came back still looking puzzled, but opened the gate and waved me on. I drove up another half-mile of blacktop, pulled up on a graveled parking area, and walked from the car to the reception lobby. There were fewer than a dozen cars in the parking lot; either their staff was incredibly small or there was another parking lot for employees tucked off in the back somewhere. *Or the employees live here,* said something in my head. Nonsense, I thought.

The reception lobby was equally quiet. Nobody there at all. A curved desk with all the paraphernalia of a busy receptionist: phones, picture screens, computer access keyboard, plush little wheeled chair. The lobby was paneled in warm woods, furnished with leather couches and chairs. There were even fresh flowers in vases on both low-slung wood slab tables. But no people.

A door in the wood paneling opened and a smiling, tall, handsomely dressed man came out. About my age, maybe a few years older. The suave public relations type: touch of gray at the temples, precise manner of speech, self-confident stride. A very *careful* man. The ideal pickpocket.

"Mr. Albano," he said in a well-modulated voice that was somewhere between a confidential whisper and a throaty tenor. "We *are* honored."

My estimation of him went up. Scratch pickpocket. He was a confidence man.

I let him shake my hand. He had a very firm, manly grip.

"My name is Peter Thornton. I'm Dr. Peña's assistant—"

"Dr. Peña?"

He almost looked hurt. "The director of this organization. Dr. Alfonso Peña. Surely Dr. Klienerman has explained—"

I cut him off with a nod. He was pumping me, and I decided to be the pumper, not the pumpee.

"Where is Dr. Peña? I'd like to see him. I don't have much time, you understand."

"Of course. Of course. But the gate guard said you were asking for Dr. Klienerman and Mr. McMurtrie."

"That's right. I'm part of the investigating team. We've got to make certain that we can handle the media from a knowledgeable basis."

"Oh, yes, certainly. That is important, isn't it?"

"Right." But we hadn't moved a centimeter from where I'd been standing all along. The door to the laboratory proper was still behind Thornton, and he was making no effort to take me through.

"This is a *very* unfortunate business," he said, lowering his voice even more.

"Yes. Now where're Klienerman and McMurtrie? And I also—"

"Dr. Klienerman left last night," Thornton said, giving me a *you should have known that* look. "He and Mr. McMurtrie went together."

"Last night?"

"By chartered plane. General Halliday insisted."

"General Halliday?" The President's father.

"Yes. They should be in Aspen by now."

Damn! That was one of the troubles with skulking off on your own. You got out of touch with everybody else. I decided to take the offensive.

"I should have been notified," I said sternly.

His eyebrows rose in alarm. "We didn't know. They didn't inform me—"

I shook my head. "There's no excuse for this kind of screw-up. I know it isn't your fault personally, but . . ."

He made a gesture that was almost like hand-wringing.

"Well," I said, "as long as I'm here, I want to meet

Dr. Peña. And I'll need to see the bodies, of course. The *bodies* are still here, aren't they?"

"Oh, yes! They've been subjected to extensive post-mortem examinations, you realize . . . but they're here."

"Let's get with it, then."

I had him on the run. He ushered me through the door and into the main building of the laboratory. We walked through miles of corridors, down stairs, through plastic-roofed ramps that connected different buildings. I got completely lost; I couldn't have found the lobby again without a troop of Boy Scouts to lead me.

We passed a strange conglomeration of sights. At first we were in an office area, obviously administrative. Rugs on the floors, neat little names and titles on the doors. Secretaries' desks placed in alcoves along the corridors. Then we stepped through one of those rampways into a different building. Here I saw workshops and what looked like chemistry laboratories: lots of glassware and bubblings and people in white smocks. Then a computer complex: more white-smocked people, but younger, mostly, and surrounded by head-high consoles with winking lights and viewscreens flashing green-glowing numbers and symbols.

Then we passed more offices, but here there were no doors, no names, no titles. The men and women inside these cubbyholes looked like researchers to me. They were scribbling equations on chalkboards or punching computer keyboards or talking animatedly with each other in words that were English but not the English language.

As we were going down a clanging flight of metal stairs, deeper into the basement levels underneath the surface building, it finally hit home in my brain that North Lake Research Laboratories was not a medical institution. It had nothing to do with medicine at all, from the looks of it.

"What's the major area of research here?" I asked Thornton.

"Em . . . biomedical," he said.

"Bio*medical?*"

"Well ... mostly biochemistry. Very advanced, of course." He produced a chuckle that was supposed to put me off my guard. "I'll tell you something. I've got a doctorate in molecular biochemistry, and I don't understand half of what these bright young people are doing nowadays."

"That far out, eh?"

I was about to ask him who paid for all these bright young people and their far-out research. But we had come to the bottom of the stairwell. There was nothing there except a blank cul-de-sac, about four paces long, with cement walls and an unmarked steel door at its end.

Thornton, looking suddenly grim, fingered the buttons of the combination lock set into the wall next to the door. It swung open and we stepped through.

This area looked medical. A large room, with pastel green walls. No windows, of course, this far underground. Glareless, pitiless overhead lights. Cold. Like a morgue, only colder. Two rollable tables in the center of the room, each bearing a body totally covered with a green sheet. Nineteen dozen different kinds of gadgets arrayed around the bodies: oscilloscopes, trays of surgical instruments, heart-lung pumps, lots of other things I didn't recognize right off.

I found myself swallowing hard. Despite the cold of the room, the stench of death was here. I went to the tables. Thornton didn't try to stop me, but I could hear his footsteps on the cold cement floor, right behind me. I stopped at the first table. So did he. I lifted a corner of the sheet.

James J. Halliday stared blankly at me. Christ, it looked *exactly* like him!

I let the sheet drop from my fingers and went to the other table. This time Thornton stayed where he was. I lifted the second sheet. The same face stared at me. The same sandy hair, the same blue eyes, the same jaw, the lips that could grin so boyishly, the broad forehead, the thin slightly beaked nose.

"I wouldn't pull the sheet any further back," Thornton's voice came from behind me, "unless you've had some surgical experience. It . . . isn't pretty."

I placed the sheet gently back on the cold face. Dammit, there were tears in my eyes. It took me a minute before I could turn back and face Thornton again.

"What were the results of the autopsies?" I asked. "What killed them?"

Thornton looked uncomfortable. "I believe Dr. Peña should discuss that with you."

"All right," I said. "Where is he?"

"He's coming down to meet you. He should have been here by now." Thornton glanced at his wrist watch.

The cold was seeping into me. "Look, couldn't we—"

"Dr. Peña is a very frail man," Thornton told me, and for the first time since I'd met him in the lobby, I got the feeling he was saying something that he really meant. "He's nearing ninety years of age. He drives himself much too hard. I hope you won't . . . say anything that will upset him."

I stared at Thornton. The life of the President of the United States was being threatened. Hell—one of those bodies could just as easily *be* James J. Halliday. And he was worried about his boss's frailties.

There wasn't time for me to answer him, though. Through a second door, one set farther back in the room than the one we had used, Dr. Peña came riding in on an electrically powered wheelchair.

He looked older than any human being I had ever seen; even Robert Wyatt would have looked coltish beside him. His face was nothing more than a death mask with incredibly lined skin stretched over the fragile bones. His head was hairless, eyes half-closed. He reminded me of the mummified remains of pharaohs; not a drop of juices left in him. He was wrapped in a heavy robe that bulged and bulked oddly. And then I saw all the cardiac and renal equipment loaded on the back rack of the wheelchair, and realized that below the neck he was probably more machine than flesh. His hands were covered with barely discernible thin plastic surgeon's gloves. It gave his long, bony fingers and the liver-spotted, tendon-ridged backs of his hands a queer filmy sheen.

His voice surprised me. It was strong, confident, alert; not at all the thin, quavering piping I had expected.

"You're the President's press secretary, are you?"

"And you're Dr. Peña," I said.

He fingered the control buttons set into the wheelchair's armrest and rolled up to me fast enough to make me involuntarily step back a pace.

"I'm a busy man, Mr. Albano. As you might suspect from looking at me, time is a very precious commodity to me. Why are you taking up my time?"

I almost grinned at him. Frail old man, my ass.

"I'm part of the team investigating . . ." I was momentarily at a loss for how to phrase it. I gestured toward the shrouded bodies.

He glowered at me. "I've already told Klienerman and that Secret Service man everything I've found out. Ask them about it."

"I will. But while we're both here, I'd like to get your opinions firsthand."

"Waste of time," he snapped.

"Why?"

"Because I have no opinions!"

"Suppose I asked you if the man sitting in the White House this morning is actually James J. Halliday?"

His breath caught on that one.

I stepped closer to him. "Is one of those . . . corpses . . . the President?"

He glanced at Thornton, then back to me. "I can only tell you that each of those corpses looks exactly like the President. Same height, same weight. Same fingerprints, retinal patterns, earlobe structure, cephalic index. Every physical determinant I have measured is precisely the same as the records Dr. Klienerman gave me for the President."

"Fingerprints," I echoed.

"Everything," he repeated. "They are physically identical to each other and to the President. They are not machines, not automata or plastic creations. They are completely human, as human as you or I. *More* human than I am, considering . . ."

"Who could produce such exact duplicates?"

Dr. Peña was silent on that one.

"Well . . . what killed them?" I asked.

His head sank onto his chest. His eyes closed.

Thornton stepped between us. "I told you not to tax him too far."

But Peña waved a feeble hand. "No . . . it is all right. I'm perfectly capable of . . . answering him."

"You should be resting," Thornton insisted.

"What killed them?" I asked again.

He gave a one-gasp laugh, a nasty accusative little snort. "What killed them? A very good question. An excellent question."

"Well? What did?"

He looked up at me, his eyes glittering with pain or hate or maybe both. "Nothing killed them. Nothing at all. No marks of violence. No poison. Not even asphyxiation. They simply died. Like marionettes whose strings have been cut. They simply fell down and . . . died."

CHAPTER SEVEN

All the way on the flight from Minneapolis to Denver I nibbled on Dr. Peña's words. *Nothing killed them ... they just fell down and ... died.* Cause of death: unknown. They just stopped living. Two adult human males who looked exactly like the President of the United States. Each died within a hundred yards of the real President. Each died of—nothing.

I was out of my league and I knew it. But something stubborn in me (or maybe something scared witless) told me to follow McMurtrie's trail. McMurtrie knew what he was doing. If he had gone to Aspen to see General Halliday, that's where I was going, too.

It's hard to believe that Aspen was once a center of the youth cult. The old city had begun as a silver miners' boom town, then rusticated for a long while, and then had become a ski resort. Kids from all over the country flocked there a couple of generations ago, to ski and loaf in the winter snows and summer sunshine. Easy living. But all things change. The kids grew up, started businesses, got respectable. Aspen became a very exclusive resort, especially after Colorado followed Nevada's lead and legalized gambling and prostitution.

Funny. Old Las Vegas had become a ghost town after the Shortage Riots of the eighties. It was really a defenseless city. When Dahlgren led his army of unemployed against the "temples of sin and gold," as he evangelistically put it, they burned the casinos and hotels to the ground. When they tried the following year to sack Denver, Morton J. Halliday, an obscure colonel in the Colorado National Guard, became a national hero. He saved Denver from the mob. He faced them down with trained, disciplined troops. And then he *fed* them, put them to work rebuilding the damage they had done in Pueblo and Albuquerque, and became the first honest-to-god hero this nation had seen since Sirica.

So now Aspen was a stronghold of the rich and the elderly, a bastion of wealth and quiet luxurious living tucked among the mighty guardian peaks of the Rockies. Las Vegas was this generation's youth center; kids lived out on the desert in communes all around the burned-out Strip, using the still-functioning solar power stations to pump up water from the deep wells.

Flying into Aspen had never improved much from the earliest days. You still had to bounce through the rough mountain air, lurching every which way while the plane's entertainment tape fed you P.R. garbage about how "the clear air makes the peaks seem much closer than they actually are."

I had white knuckles and sweaty palms all through the forty-minute flight. By the time we landed, my stomach was in a mess. It calmed down a bit on the taxi ride to the Halliday enclave.

You didn't just drop in on General Halliday. Not even if you worked in the White House. He ruled this area—the whole state of Colorado, in fact—from his mansion on Red Peak—the Western White House, when his son was home. When James J. had first become governor of Colorado, most political pundits had assumed that he was just a front man for his powerful father. They got several stunning surprises when James proved to be his own man. You couldn't predict the Governor's behavior by finding out what the General wanted. This caused some towering arguments between them. I'd seen a few that raged from cocktails through dawn.

The taxi dropped me off at the gate house, a solid stone, pitched roof, four-story building that could have held a couple of Swiss chalets and Fort Apache inside it. Actually, it quartered most of the General's security staff. Many of the older men had been the scared young troopers who'd made a hero out of the General back in Denver. And there was enough new blood to take on the state police, it seemed to me.

A helicopter droned past as I crunched along the gravel walkway up to the guardhouse's front door. The reception area was sliced into two spaces: a small lobby just inside the door, where visitors stand, and, on the other side of a transparent bulletproof screen, a much larger area staffed mostly by women sitting at desks, phone switchboards, and television monitoring devices.

The girl at the desk closest to the partition looked up as the door closed silently behind me.

"Yessir, can I help you?" She had a pleasant smile, the kind they teach you in those schools that specialize in getting ahead in the world.

I told her my name, and she recognized who I was almost instantly. The "almost" was a glance at the little computer viewscreen on her desk. Fast computer, with deep personnel files.

It took only a few minutes for her to phone the main house, then smile up at me again and tell me that a car would pick me up outside in a few minutes. I thanked her and went outside to bask in the spring sunshine.

Snow was still banked deep around the building, but the sun was warm and birds were chirping cheerfully in the newly leafing trees. I walked across the cleared gravel-covered parking area to the lip of the trail. You could see the whole valley from up here, sparkling in the snow like a picture in a tourist brochure. The air *was* clear, and clean. I remembered nights up here when I had first started working for The Man, going out for long walks with him. We'd start out talking about R & D policy and end up stargazing.

The car came and I was driven to the main house. The driver took me inside and ushered me into a library: dark woods; ceiling-high bookshelves covering three walls, except for a stone fireplace; windows on the fourth wall overlooking a pine forest. The fireplace was empty, although the room was comfortably warm. I paced between the easy chairs in front of the hearth and the couch alongside the windows.

The door opened, and Robert Wyatt stepped into the room. I felt my mouth open in surprise.

"I thought you were in Washington."

He looked annoyed, thin lips pressed tight. "I could say the same for you."

"I'm looking for McMurtrie. I told the woman at the gate house that he's the one I want to see."

"Too late," His Holiness said.

My stomach clenched. "What do you mean?"

"He just 'coptered out of here, going back to Denver and then to Washington."

"Oh."

For a few heartbeats we stood facing each other, me by the windows, His Holiness across the room, only three paces from the door. Between us was a Persian carpet, glowing red and gold where the sun streaked across it.

"What did you want with McMurtrie?" Wyatt asked me.

Good question. What could I answer? *I wanted him to hold my hand and tell me everything's going to be okay.* I said, "I want to stay on top of this investigation. I decided to stick with him. This is too big . . ."

"How did you know he was here?"

"Dr. Peña told me."

Wyatt's head actually jerked back a few centimeters. The vein in his forehead pulsed. "You were at North Lake? When?"

"This morning . . ." Which reminded me. "Robert, I haven't had anything to eat all damned day. How about a sandwich or something?"

He almost looked as if he were going to say no. Instead, "Wait here. I think the General will want to see you."

So I waited. I sat at the desk near the door and

phoned Vickie, told her where I was. She looked funny; not upset, really, but kind of tense.

"You all right?" I asked her.

"Oh, I'm fine," she said. "It's you I'm worrying about. Hunter's getting to enjoy talking with the President and briefing the press corps. He'll probably want to move into your office by tomorrow morning."

"Let him," I said.

"Be serious." She was. Her elfin face was as close to grimness as it could get. On anyone else it would look like the beginnings of a smile.

"Okay. Serious," I said. "Get me a rundown on Dr. Alfonso Peña. College degrees, career, the whole *curriculum vitae*. And a rundown on North Lake Research Laboratories. I want to know where they get their money from."

"You ended a sentence with a preposition," she said.

"Arrant nonsense, up with which—"

"—I shall not put," Vickie quoted with me. We laughed together.

"All right. I'll be back in the office tomorrow. Have that information ready for me early. And tell Hunter to hold off on moving his office furniture."

The door to the library opened and Wyatt came in, followed by a self-driven cart loaded with lunch.

"To hear is to obey," Vickie was saying.

I glanced at the food, then back to the phone screen. "Hey," I said to her, "you're supposed to smile when you say that."

She made a smile, but it didn't look very convincing.

"I'll see you tomorrow," I said.

"Call me if your plans change, will you?"

"Okay. Will do."

I clicked off and turned to Wyatt. "The General still sets a good table."

"There's beer in the refrigerator section," he said, "underneath the tablecloth on your side."

"Terrific."

We were halfway through our first sandwiches when the General strode into the library.

Morton J. Halliday looked as though he were in uniform even when he was wearing an old corduroy shirt and faded chinos, his costume at that moment. He was tall, with an imperious look to his eyes, a haughty nose, and an iron-gray mustache. His hair was clipped short, in time-honored military style, and nearly all white now. He didn't show the least sign of baldness, something he teased Wyatt about on those rare occasions when he'd had enough to drink to let down his self-control a little.

He had the mien and style of an emperor, and some of his very oldest friends—like Wyatt—could recall when the General had first married and quietly proclaimed to his closest associates that he was going to father a President. He'd done exactly that, even though his wife had died while the son was an infant and he had raised James J. by himself.

Not exactly single-handed, of course. But the General had never let James J. wander far from this mountain stronghold on Red Peak. Instead, he brought the world to the boy. The best scholars on the planet tutored James. Local gossip had it that there were more Nobel Prize laureates on Red Peak at any given moment during the boy's schooling years than anywhere else on earth. The General bought the Aspen Institute and gave it to his son as a sixteenth birthday present. And when James did travel, it was with a security team as large and dedicated as the Secret Service guards for the President. It was like a small army traveling. He was born to be President, and he started living like one so far back in his childhood that he had taken to living in the White House as if it were his natural habitat.

There were always those who tried to find the strings that controlled James J. Halliday. The obvious link was from his father to the banking, mineral, and industrial interests that the General was tied to. I have to confess that my own first interest in Governor Halliday, the dark horse candidate for the Presidency, was exactly for that reason. I was going to find his feet of clay. I was going to expose his connections with the oil and banking and God-knows-what other big-money manipulators who were using him as a front man. I was going to knock him down. The son of a bitch had stolen Laura from me.

I never found those links. They just weren't there. Halliday was his own man, as fiercely independent and tough-minded as his hero father. Despite myself, I liked the man. I wound up working for him, of course. And the relationship between James and his father reminded me of the relationship between the ancient conqueror Alexander the Great and his father, Philip of Macedon: pride, love, competition, maybe envy. Philip had been assassinated, probably on order of his son.

Now the General stood before me, saber-straight and lean. He fixed me with his eyes as I was about to take a bite of my half-finished sandwich. I felt like a very small mouse that had just been spotted by a very hungry cat.

"Just what in hell is going on?" he said. He didn't raise his voice. He didn't have to. There was enough iron even in his calmest tones to swing a compass needle around.

A slice of tomato oozed out of my sandwich as I replied, "Good afternoon, General." Dazzling comeback.

He strode over to our table. Wyatt got up and fetched a chair for him. I got to my feet.

As we all sat down, the General asked me, "Are you supposed to be the President's press secretary, or some amateur detective out of a lousy TV show?"

I let the rest of my sandwich drop into the plate. "Is that a riddle or do you want a serious answer?"

He glared at Wyatt, as if it were *his* fault, then returned to me. "Listen, sonny, you're supposed to be working in Washington. What in the name of hell are you doing running around the countryside to Minnesota and up here?"

"I'm trying to find out what's going on, and who's attempting to kill your son."

"We have the whole mother-thumping FBI and Secret Service available for that. Plus the Army, Navy, and Aerospace Force, if we need 'em. Who the hell gave you a sheriff's badge?"

I took a deep breath. *His bark's worse than his bite,* I told myself, even though I didn't believe it. "General Halliday . . . sir. It may come as a shock to you, but I cannot, and will not, try to keep this story away from the news hounds unless I know *exactly* what the story is. I'm not going to operate in the dark."

Wyatt smirked. "And how much have you found out by running up to Minnesota?"

"At least I know as much about what killed those duplicates as Dr. Peña does."

"You met Peña?" the General snapped.

"Yes."

"And what did he tell you?"

"Not a helluva lot. Said he can't determine what killed the duplicates. Apparently they just keeled over and died."

"That's the same report we got," Wyatt said. "And the same information you would have gotten, if you'd been in your office this morning."

"Really?" I asked.

His Holiness clenched his teeth and said nothing.

I turned back to the General. "Why was McMurtrie here? Did he bring Dr. Klienerman with him?"

Now it was the General's turn to keep his mouth clamped shut. He looked at Wyatt and cocked an eyebrow.

"The first . . . body," Wyatt said, his voice chokingly strained, "was found in Denver. McMurtrie figured as long as he was coming that close, he might as well drop in here and tell us what was going on."

"He knew you were here?" I asked Wyatt.

"We were in constant communication all the time," he answered.

"What's Dr. Klienerman have to say about all this?"

"Nothing," the General snapped. "Not a damned thing."

"He and Dr. Peña didn't get along very well," Wyatt explained. "You know how it is when two prima donnas get under the same roof."

"What do you mean?"

Wyatt looked even more uncomfortable. "Peña wouldn't allow Klienerman to see the bodies of the duplicates."

"What? But he's the President's personal physician! If one of those bodies *is* the President . . ."

"They're not," said the General.

"How can you be certain?"

"Peña's satisfied . . ."

"Dr. Peña told me they were exactly alike, for Chrissake!" I knew I was shouting, but there wasn't much I could do about it. "He can't tell one from the other, and he can't tell either one from the President's medical profile."

"They are not the President," the General insisted.

I took a good look at him. Arguing with him on that point would have been like trying to tear down Red Peak with a soggy toothpick. He had made up his mind and that was that.

Wyatt said, "Meric, you really ought to get back to Washington and stay close to your office. We'll keep you informed."

"I still want to see McMurtrie," I said.

"That will be impossible," the General said.

"Why can't—"

"McMurtrie's helicopter crashed between here and Mt. Evans. I got the word just before I came in here."

I couldn't move. Not even my mouth would work. It was like being paralyzed.

Wyatt seemed stunned, too. But only for a moment. He asked, "McMurtrie . . . ?"

"Dead. Everybody on board was killed. McMurtrie, Klienerman and the pilot."

"They're sure?"

The General's voice was stony. "State police helicopter flew over the crash site. Heard a distress call and went to investigate. By the time they got there, there was nothing to see but burning wreckage. No survivors."

"Jesus-suffering-Christ," said Wyatt.

I still couldn't utter a word. But my brain was racing at hyperkinetic speed. *McMurtrie was killed. Murdered. Either he or Klienerman had found something, and they were both killed before they could tell anyone. Murdered by somebody here in the General's household.*

CHAPTER EIGHT

It was around midnight when my flight landed at Washington National. *Home of the brave,* I told myself. It was an effort just to pull myself out of the seat and trudge past the weary stewardesses standing at the plane's main hatch. Even their conditioned-reflex smiles looked bedraggled. I felt as if that helicopter of the General's had landed on my back. Utterly tired. Not just physically. The kind of nothing-left feeling when you've burned up the last of your adrenalin and the monster you were facing is still there, bigger than ever, breathing fire and reaching out to clutch you.

The airport was just about deserted. They stopped flights into National after midnight. The official reason was the noise; it bothered people living in the area. The real reason was security. Ever since the National Vigilance Society had tried to seize the Government and the city a dozen years ago, the airport had been kept under *very* tight security guard.

The damned corridor out to the main terminal building seemed endless. It was like a surrealistic nightmare; I was walking alone up this gradually sloping bare white-tiled corridor, scared to look behind me for fear that whoever got McMurtrie would be coming after me, scared to push ahead because I *knew* there were things in that city out there that I'd rather not face up to.

But as I went past the deserted passenger inspection station, with its X-ray cameras for searching baggage and its magnetic detectors for finding metal on passengers, the whole gloomy airport lit up for me. Vickie was sitting there, reading a magazine.

I was the first of the half-dozen passengers coming out of the plane, and she hadn't looked up yet to notice anyone approaching. Her golden hair was a touch of sun warmth in the impersonal coldness of the terminal building. She was dressed casually in slacks and sweater, but she looked grand to me.

"You don't get paid overtime, you know," I said.

She looked up, startled momentarily, and then grinned. "I happened to be in the neighborhood . . ." She got up and stuffed the magazine into her shoulder bag.

"How'd you know which flight I'd be on?"

"Checked with Denver." She looked very pleased with herself. "I may not have started life as a newspaper reporter, but I know how to find things out when I want to."

"You ended a sentence with a preposition," I said.

"The hell I did."

We walked together out past the empty, echoing baggage carousels, mindlessly turning even though there was no luggage on any of them. The traffic rotary outside the terminal, so noisy and bustling all day long, was dark and quiet now. I didn't see a cab anywhere.

"I've got my car," Vickie said, pointing toward the parking area on the other side of the rotary.

"I didn't know you had a car." It was a little chilly in the night air. The sky was clouded over, although a quarter moon glowed through the overcast dimly.

"Well, it's not really mine. It belongs to a friend. He's out of town and I'm minding it for him."

I didn't reply. We walked straight across the rotary, just like Boston pedestrians, marching across six traffic lanes, a big circle of withered grass, and six more lanes on the other side. The parking area was automated. We got into the car—a thoroughly battered old gas burner that roared and coughed when Vickie started it up—and drove out, stopping only to pay the parking fee at the unattended gate.

"You didn't walk around here in the dark by yourself," I said.

"Sure. It's okay . . . the place is really deserted. And they've got television monitors watching everything. The guards would have come out of the terminal building if anyone had bothered me."

"Just in time to join the gang bang," I muttered.

"Worried about my honor?" she asked as she turned onto the bridge that led across the Potomac.

"Worried about your life."

"I can take care of myself. I've never been raped yet."

"Once is enough, from what I hear."

She grimaced. "I suppose you're right."

By the time we had pulled up in front of my apartment building, she had told me all about the car and its owner. The engine had been converted to hydrogen fuel, which is why the old five-seat sedan was now a two-seater. The rest was fuel tank. Very bulky. And highly flammable.

"But don't worry," Vickie assured me. "Ron tells me the tank is very crashworthy."

"I'm thrilled."

Ron was a staffer for a Congressman from Kentucky. A very likeable hillbilly with a passion for cars, the way Vickie described him. I could feel my lip curl in contempt, in the darkness of the car. Twanging accent and the brains of a grease monkey, I thought.

"I met him at a car rally in Bethesda last year," Vickie said. "We go to lots of races and rallies."

"I didn't know you were a car freak," I said.

"There's a lot about me you don't know," she answered as she pulled the stick shift back into parking gear. "Well . . . here you are. Door-to-door service."

"Come on up," I said. "Least I can do is make you a drink. Or some coffee."

She shook her head slightly. "I can't leave the car here. They'll ticket it."

"So what? I'll pull rank and get it taken care of. Old Boston tradition."

"They might tow it."

"So let them. I'll get it back before your hillbilly friend returns to town."

She really looked perplexed. "Meric . . . I don't fuck with the boss."

I guess that was supposed to stop me, or warn me, or turn me off. Instead, I heard myself reply, "Don't worry about it. The whole apartment's protected by TV cameras. If I attack you, guards will spring out of the walls and beat my balls off."

She laughed. A good, hearty, full-throated laugh. "All right, all right. As long as we understand each other."

"Sure we do." I was only half lying.

She did take coffee instead of a drink. I poured myself a couple thumbs of Scotch. Vickie sat on the chrome and leather rocker in my living room. I sprawled tiredly on the sofa.

After a sip of the Scotch I asked her, "What made you come out to the airport for me?"

"I'm not sure," she said. She started to look for a place to put the coffee mug down, settled for the rug. "I guess I was curious to find out what you've been up to—what's bugging you, and what all this interest in that laboratory in Minnesota's about. I'm usually a late-night person anyway; never get to bed before one or two. So I thought I'd give you a surprise at the airport."

"It was damned nice of you," I said. "Nothing lonelier than getting off a late flight with nobody there to greet you."

"I know," she said. "You told me that once . . . in the office."

"I did?" But instead of continuing that line of conversation, she bent down and took the coffee mug again.

"How's everything been in the office the past few days?" I asked, changing the subject.

"Mostly routine. Hunter's doing a good job, and the press is bending over backward to avoid any unusual treatment that might get interpreted as racist. Oh, you got a call from a Mr. Ryan, of the Boston *News-Globe*. He said you invited him down for an interview."

"He invited himself."

"I think Greta set him up with a tentative date next Monday."

"Okay. That sounds good."

We chatted for a few minutes more, and then she got up to leave. I'm not sure how it happened, but I wound up standing in front of the door, holding her hands in mine, and saying, "Don't go. Stay awhile longer."

"No, Meric . . . really . . ."

"Couple nights ago, on the phone, you said you wished you were with me."

"That was . . ." She looked away, then back at me, her eyes the color of a tropical lagoon. "It's not fair to remember what I say when . . . well, it's not fair."

"Vickie . . . please. I don't want to be alone."

"Neither do I."

"Well, then."

"I told you," she said, her voice rising a notch, "I don't screw around with the boss."

I didn't let go of her. "Listen. Tomorrow I'm the boss. Tonight I'm a guy who wants you . . . who needs you."

"What are you frightened of?" she asked.

I started to answer, but held it back.

"Something's pursuing you, Meric. Something's got you terrified. What is it?"

"Nothing that concerns you."

"But maybe I can help . . ."

I shook my head and let her hands go. "No, Vickie. You don't want to know. Believe me. You're better off not knowing."

She put a hand to my cheek. "My God, Meric. You're trembling!"

I pulled away from her.

"It's about Laura Halliday, isn't it? I wish you could feel that much passion for me."

"It's not her," I snapped. "And it's not passion ... it's fear. Just plain chickenshit cold sweat fear."

"Fear? Of what?"

I slumped back onto the sofa and she came and sat beside me. "Meric, what's happening? What are you so frightened of? Don't I have a right to know?"

"No. You don't. Dammit, Vick ... I'm trying to protect you. As long as you don't know anything about it, you're safe."

"Safe from what?"

"They killed McMurtrie," I blurted. "Dr. Klienerman, too. Made it look like an accident."

"They? Who?"

"General Halliday, maybe. Or Wyatt. Or person or persons unknown. I don't know who! I don't know why. But I might be on their list, too. And at the top of the goddamned list is the President."

Her eyes widened.

"I've already told you more than it's safe for you to know," I said. "Now get out while the getting's good. Go back to California and become a stock car racer. It's a helluva lot safer and cleaner than what's going on around here."

I would have made a lousy intelligence agent. Vickie got the whole story out of me, bit by bit. The more I swore I wasn't going to say any more, the more I warned her that I was looking out for her own safety, the more I blabbered about the whole ugly business. A part of my mind watched the fiasco in disgust, while another part felt immense relief that I had somebody to talk to, somebody to share the whole incredible burden of doubts and fears. *And anyway,* I rationalized, *between the fact that she works for you and you phoned her from General Halliday's place, and she met you at the airport and drove you home, they probably figure she knows as much as you do.*

By the time I'd finished talking, we were both drinking Scotch and looking very sober and scared.

"Then there's nobody you can go to?" Vickie asked at last.

I shrugged. "McMurtrie was the one guy I trusted. He's out of it now."

"What are you going to do?"

"Wish to hell I knew." I finished my glass, turned and saw that the bottle was empty. "There's one thing I can do . . . the only thing I can think of."

"What's that?"

"Blow it wide open. Tell the press. Make the whole mess public."

She thought a moment. Then, slowly, "If you did that . . ."

"I know. It'd paralyze the whole Government. Bring all of Washington to a standstill. Cripple everything. Maybe shake the whole damned Government apart and send us over the edge, once and for all."

Vickie said, "I wasn't thinking of that."

"What, then?"

"If you tried to make it public, they'd have to try to kill you, too."

There it was. It wasn't just me being paranoid. Vickie saw it, too. I could be on their list. Hell, I *was* on their list. I knew it.

"What are you going to do about it?" she asked.

"Nothing," I said. "Not a goddamned thing. And if they've got this apartment bugged, I sure as hell hope they hear that. I'm not going to blow any whistles until I'm convinced that it'd do more good than harm."

"How will you decide?"

"Damned if I know. Guess I'll have to talk to The Man and see what his reactions are. From there on, it's anybody's ball game."

She gave me a long, grave look. "You could go away. You could resign and leave the country. Make certain that it's obvious you're getting out of the game."

I thought about it for a moment. "Maybe . . . except that . . . hell, I can't. It wouldn't do any good. They'd still be after the President, and I'd just be letting them get away with it."

Vickie said nothing, but I somehow got the feeling that my answer was the one she had wanted to hear.

We ended up in bed together. The Scotch finally took effect, and I don't remember too much of it, except that it was terrific and she liked to be on top. Which was fine with me. The last real memory I have of that night is of our two sweaty bodies plunging in rhythm, her firm little breasts bobbing above me and her knees clamping my torso tight. We forgot about a lot of things before dawn broke.

CHAPTER NINE

The next couple of days are just blurs in my mind. I went through the office routine mechanically, numbly, my mind in such a turmoil that it's a wonder I could find my desk or get my boots on straight. Greta clucked over me and did everything she could, including sending me home with a jar of homemade chicken soup. She thought I was coming down with a virus.

The President seemed calm and unruffled. When I asked him about McMurtrie he turned grim for a few minutes, but as far as I could fathom from him and Wyatt, the investigation was still being kept small, quiet, and ultratight.

Vickie was . . . well, Vickie. That one night was one night. In the office we were boss and assistant. She was as pleasant and helpful as always. I guess I was polite and reasonable. She didn't act coy or betrayed. I asked her out to dinner, she accepted, and we ended the night at her door. "Don't get possessive about me," she said. I felt relieved and annoyed, both at once.

We drew an almost total blank in our search for information about North Lake Labs and Dr. Peña.

"He's almost a nonperson," she complained tiredly, after several days of searching the records. "There's his file from Princeton, more than forty years ago. There's a couple of brief mentions of his attending meetings of biochemists and other scientific groups, but nothing at all later than the early seventies. Somebody's done a very thorough job of keeping him out of sight."

"Or erasing the records," I said.

Her eyes went round. "They couldn't be *that* thorough, could they?"

I had no real answer. "What about North Lake Labs?"

"Very hush-hush," Vickie said. "Deep military secrecy. Restricted-access list and all that. We'd have to go through the Secretary of Defense's office or the Senate Armed Services Committee."

"And we can't do that without advertising the fact that we're snooping," I said.

"It could be dangerous for you. But maybe not for me. Maybe they don't realize . . ."

"Uh-uh." I wagged a finger at her. "Dangerous for anybody. Stay clear or you'll wind up in some godforsaken ravine, like McMurtrie and Klienerman."

Vickie fidgeted unhappily in her chair. "Then what in hell do we *do*, Meric?"

"Nothing. Not a goddamned thing. We sit and wait. And think."

"For how long?"

I shrugged. "It's Friday. I've got to talk with Len Ryan on Monday. I'll make up my mind by then."

"It's going to be a long weekend for you," she said.

"Yeah. Think I'll drive out into the country. That ought to be the best place to get some thinking done."

"Out to Camp David?"

"No, I don't want to be with the President this weekend. I'll go the other way, maybe down to Virginia Beach."

"I've still got the car," Vickie said.

I shook my head. "You stay clear of me for the time being. If I make it past Monday, then we can talk."

She started to argue, but I made noises like a boss and got her to leave the office. I don't think she was sore, but if anything was going to happen that weekend, I didn't want her around to get caught by the blast.

It was almost quitting time when the phone call

came. Greta had just stuck her head into my office to announce that she was taking off fifteen minutes early to beat the traffic crunch. She did that every Friday, and she always made that announcement, and I always nodded my head.

Phone calls from the President weren't all that unusual. When he had first taken office, The Man began making spot calls to anyone and everyone, just checking on how things were going down on the working levels, sampling morale, seeing who looked guilty or busy or happy or pissed off. The standard joke was that if your phones beeped out "Ruffles and Flourishes" instead of buzzing, you knew who was calling.

My phone just buzzed. I touched the ON button, and The Man's face appeared on my desk screen.

"Hello, Meric," he said pleasantly.

"Mr. President."

"Do you have any plans for the weekend?" he asked.

It had been an hour or so since my conversation with Vickie. "Nothing special. Why do you ask?"

He smiled. "Laura and I were wondering if you could have dinner with us tomorrow evening. Nothing formal. Just a quiet evening. The three of us."

"I thought you were going to Maryland for the weekend."

"That's canceled. Too much work to do. I'm staying here for the weekend."

"You might have informed your press secretary about your switch in plans. I've got to make sure the press corps—"

"Meric," he said with a patient grin, "I *am* informing my press secretary. I just made up my mind about it a few minutes ago. And Laura thought it'd been quite a while since we broke bread together, quietly and informally. Can you make it or not?"

"Yessir, I can make it. Of course."

"Good. Seven o'clock. Bring an appetite."

"Right. Thank you."

I wish I could say that the first thing I did after

clicking off the phone was to check my office for electronic bugs or call Vickie and tell her that if anything happened to me she should break the story to the media. I didn't. I tore madly out of the office and down the hallway to catch Greta before she got into the elevator and away. I needed her to start the machinery of informing the press corps about the President's change in plans. Otherwise they'd have my hide on the door by morning.

I just missed her. I had to grab a couple of the younger workers and draft them for the emergency. It took more than an hour to make certain that the entire press corps had been informed.

Even before Halliday had turned the White House into his almost totally private preserve, tourists had never been allowed up onto the second floor, where the President and his family had their living quarters. Halliday was obsessive about his privacy, to the point where foreign dignitaries were no longer even occasionally put up in the White House. They stayed at Blair House or some other nearby building. Tourists still plodded through the ground and first floors of the Presidential mansion, but the second floor was sacrosanct, even to Cabinet members and most of the President's personal staff.

That's why on Saturday I took my usual route through the underground slideway to the West Wing and came up just outside the Oval Office. Saturday or not, Mrs. Bester was at her desk; the rumor among the staff was that she never budged from her post, and her swivel chair had a potty under it. She was a tough old broad; at least she looked that way. But on the inside, she was even tougher. Which is what the President wanted in his private secretary.

I could hear voices coming from inside the Oval Office.

"Is he in there?" I asked cautiously. Somehow she always intimidated me.

"Yes," she said. Nothing more. She never volunteered information. She just sat behind her fortress-sized desk, gazing at me through steely eyes.

"He . . . uh, he's expecting me."

Looking as if she'd never believe such a transparent lie, she buzzed on the intercom. I couldn't hear what the President was saying to her; the receiver was jewel-sized and tucked into her left ear.

"You can go in," she said at last, still looking as if she were very dubious about the whole arrangement.

The President was looking very grim, sitting ramrod straight in his desk chair, his hands flat on the desk top. Admiral Del Bello, the Chairman of the Joint Chiefs of Staff, was sitting equally stiffly in front of the desk. The Admiral was in civvies, but you could still see the gold braid all over him.

"Meric," the President shot before I could get the door closed, "what would be the public reaction to our sending the Third Fleet into the Persian Gulf?"

I blinked.

"Not just the Third Fleet," the Admiral said, in a voice like steel cable twanging. "With all our budgetary cutbacks, the Third's more of a paper fleet than a real one. We'd need—"

The President cut him off with an impatient gesture. "Come on, Meric. I don't want a computer analysis. Just your gut reaction."

My gut reaction was to take a deep breath first. Then, "Well, Mr. President, I think you'd get a strong split in public opinion. A lot of people will be dead-set against our getting sucked into the Shah's war, and a lot of others will think we ought to go in there and grab the oil fields while we can."

"You see?" Admiral Del Bello crowed. "There would be substantial public support . . . sir."

"And considerable casualties," The Man retorted. "And we'd turn Iran into an enemy, drive the Shah off the throne, and let the Russians overthrow all our diplomatic successes in the area. The entire Middle East would hate us. Even Israel."

"But we'd have the oil!" the Admiral said, clenching his fists excitedly. "Mr. President, we'd have the oil fields! We could take the entire Arabian peninsula."

The President cocked an eye at him. "Like we took Southeast Asia? No, thank you, Admiral."

Del Bello was not one to surrender gracefully. "Mr. President, I really think you should allow the Joint Chiefs to have their day in court. They're waiting for you in Camp David."

He shook his head.

The Admiral's face reddened. "Mr. President! It is our duty to advise you on military matters. The plan we have worked out—"

"What happens to the Third Fleet if the Iranians use nuclear weapons in the Persian Gulf? You can't disperse your ships widely enough to keep the casualties down to an acceptable rate, can you? The fleet would be demolished."

"Mr. President . . ."

"Well? Isn't that true? Or am I wrong?"

Shifting in his chair, the Admiral said, "But if we . . ."

The President leaned forward and jabbed a finger at his top military adviser. "The fleet would be demolished, would it not?"

"There's always that possibility. Yessir."

"And what happens if we succeed in taking the Kuwait fields and knocking out the Iranian forces? What will the USSR do? Invade Iran? Attack our men? The Russians won't allow us to gobble up the Middle East."

His face red-splotched, the Admiral said, "Sir, I'd rather not discuss such highly classified matters with your press secretary present. There's more information that I want to present to you, and . . ."

The President eased back in his chair and smiled at me. "All right. Meric, would you mind letting us finish this in private? Mrs. Halliday is upstairs having a cocktail. I'd appreciate it if you'd keep her company for a few minutes more."

"Certainly, Mr. President," I said.

I got as far as the door before he asked, "Oh, Meric. One further question. What would be the public reaction to a Russian ultimatum that we either quit the Persian Gulf or suffer an ICBM attack?"

I turned back. The Admiral's face had gone purple. The President seemed quite cheerful. "Never mind," he told me, waving me out the door. "You don't have to answer that one. I know what the reaction would be."

Only a cretin could fail to find his way down the West Wing corridor, into the main elevator, and up to the second floor. But I had a security guard escort me all the way. Standard operating procedure. The man was as silent as a well-oiled robot. The guard ushered me through the Yellow Room, with its Dolly Madison furniture, and out onto the Truman porch.

Laura was sitting there alone, stretched out on a recliner in shorts and halter, watching the sunset and listening to the birds getting ready for nightfall. She had a tall drink beside her.

She looked up at me. "Hello again, Meric."

"Hello," I said. "The President said he'll be tied up a few minutes more with Admiral Del Bello."

With a smile she asked, "The Admiral hasn't had a stroke yet?"

"He's getting close to it." I pulled up the nearest webchair and sat next to her.

"You need a drink," Laura said. "Tequila and lime, isn't it?"

"Dry sherry . . . amontillado, preferably."

She looked at me, and I tried to stay cool. "You've changed," she said.

"That's right."

Laura touched the phone keyboard on the serving table next to her recliner. "You look uptight, Meric."

"Look," I blurted, "it'd be a lot easier for all of us if we stopped playing games. I was in love with you. Maybe I still am. Let's not act like it never happened."

Her face went serious, almost scared.

"Okay," I went on. "So what do you want this time? To find out if I'm still loyal to him? If I'm going to keep the lid on this thing?"

"It's important."

"It's cost four lives," I snapped. "Five. I forgot about the helicopter pilot. McMurtrie was a damned good man—"

"I know that better than you do."

It was the President. I jumped to my feet as he slowly walked out onto the porch. He looked at Laura.

"You shouldn't be wearing that. Not here. This isn't Key West."

She made a sly smile. "There's nothing to worry about. Even if some news photographer got close enough to snap a picture, Meric would pull the right wires to keep it from being published. Wouldn't you, Meric?"

"That's not what I came here to talk about," I said.

"You're here," the President said, "because I told you to come here."

I felt a shock inside me. He sounded more like his father than himself. He was blazingly angry, for some reason. Down in the Oval Office, even though he was arguing strongly with Del Bello, he could smile. But now he was radiating anger.

"You were talking about McMurtrie," the President said to me.

"That's right. And four other dead men."

"What about them?"

I'd never seen him this way before. Was he sore about Laura? Maybe it had been her idea to invite me over here and he didn't like it.

"Mr. President . . . do you still want me to keep quiet about the attempts on your life?"

He stood straight and rigid in front of me. Not the usual relaxed slouch, not at all. "As far as I know," he answered stiffly, "there have been no attempts on my life."

I couldn't believe I'd heard him right. "No attempts . . . ?"

"Two imposters have been found, both dead of unknown causes. A helicopter accident has killed the chief of my personal security force and my personal physician. No one has fired a shot at me; no one has made any attempt whatsoever on me."

"And the investigation on those two . . . imposters? Who's taking that over, with McMurtrie dead?"

"Robert Wyatt is handling that. We'll be using selected personnel from the Secret Service and the FBI."

"And you want me to keep it all under wraps?"

"I *expect* you to keep everything quiet, until I'm ready to make a public announcement."

"And when will that be?"

"Maybe never. If we find out who's responsible for those duplicates, and the story's sensitive enough, you might never get to tell the press about it."

About the only thing I could say was, "I see."

"Now I need to know, Meric," he went on, deathly cold now, "if I can count on your cooperation and your help. There's no reason for you to play detective in this. We have enough experts for that. We'll find out who's behind these killings. What I need from you is silence. Or your resignation. Which will it be?"

It was like getting punched between the eyes. I bet I staggered backwards a step or two. "My resignation? You're asking for . . ."

"I'm asking you to decide. I don't want you to resign. But I've got to have absolute loyalty and cooperation. There's no third possibility."

"I see," I said again.

"You can think it over for a day or so. Sleep on it. Let me know Monday."

"No need to," I heard myself say. "I'll stick. I'll get the job done."

"You're sure?"

For the first time in my life, I was knowingly lying about something important. But I had the feeling that if I resigned, a fatal accident might hit me, too. And moreover, if Halliday was starting to purge his staff of everyone except blindly loyal followers, something ugly was going on.

"I'm sure," I said. "As long as you have Wyatt keep me informed on the progress of the investigation. I still have to know what I should avoid stepping on in front of the press."

He nodded once, curtly. "Good. I'll go in and phone Robert right now. I'll tell him that you're still on the team, and he should cooperate with you."

"Fine. Thank you."

"Meet me in the dining room," he said.

My drink arrived as the President left the balcony. Laura excused herself to dress for dinner. I sipped sherry and knew what it felt like to be a politician. I had said one thing and meant something else altogether. *One slip-up, though, and he'll know where you stand,* I thought. *And when that happens, you won't be standing for long.*

But by the time we'd gathered together in the President's Dining Room, with its wallpaper depicting wildly inaccurate scenes from the American Revolution, The Man was his old cheerful, relaxed self again. He even joked about how grim-faced I looked.

It wasn't until the dinner was over and I was sitting in the dark rear seat of a White House limousine on my way back to my apartment that I realized the entire truth of it. *He's in on it. Whatever's going on, the President is not one of the intended victims of the plot; he's the chief plotter!*

CHAPTER TEN

I never did go out to the country. I stayed holed up in my apartment, thinking, worrying, wondering what to do. I couldn't sleep Saturday night after that dinner with The Man and Laura. I paced my three rooms all Sunday morning, then started cleaning the place, desperate for something to occupy my time and fidgety hands. I wondered briefly if any of the neighbors would complain about the vacuum running so early in the day, or cause a fuss with the cleaning service and its union. But everyone else in the building must have either been out at church or sleeping soundly; the phone didn't buzz once.

By midafternoon I was trying to force myself to watch a baseball game on television. Even in three dimensions it bored hell out of me. I couldn't concentrate on it. My mind kept circling back to the same thoughts, the same fears, the same conclusions. *If he's in on it, then Laura must be, too.* I wanted to believe otherwise, but I knew that was a stupid straw to clutch at. *She's part of it.*

Part of what? What in hell is the President trying to do with men made to look exactly like him? Why was McMurtrie murdered? Was there a power struggle going on? A coup?

Have they—whoever they are—already slipped their man into the White House? No. That much I was certain of. They could make somebody look exactly like the President, but not behave so minutely similar to him. Despite that little show of real rage on the back

103

porch Saturday evening, The Man was still James J. Halliday, not a duplicate. Of that I was certain.

But why is he behaving this way? Why so secretive about it? All right, keep it out of the press. That stands to reason. But most of the White House staff didn't know about this. Certainly the Cabinet didn't. Nor the Vice-President. I wondered if even the FBI had been told about it. There would've been rumors and rumbles all over town if more than eleven people were in on the investigation. Even after McMurtrie and Klienerman were killed, the only chatter was the "too bad, they were good men" kind of talk that follows every accidental death.

Who's trying to get rid of the President? And why is The Man keeping the battle so tightly under wraps?

My apartment was spotless and even the laundry was done by the time the answer hit me. I was standing in the middle of the living room, looking for something else to do, trying to keep myself occupied. The sun was low in the west, sending red-gold streams of light through my windows. The TV set was blathering mindlessly: some game show. And the answer hit me.

The General.

The man who had raised his son to be President, but got a President whom he didn't agree with. The man who grew more paranoid and megalomaniacal each day. The closer he came to death, the more wild-eyed he got about "setting the country straight." And if his son couldn't do the job the way the General wanted it done, then the General would make a new son and put *him* in the White House.

It sounded crazy. But it fit. That's why the President wouldn't come out with all guns firing against his shadowy opponent. That's why McMurtrie was killed just after talking to the General. And Dr. Klienerman—he had probably recognized the symptoms right off.

The dramatic thing to have done would have been to phone the White House immediately and pledge my support to The Man wholeheartedly. Instead, I simply took a frozen dinner out of the refrigerator and popped it into the microwave cooker. There were three things wrong with my terrific piece of deduction.

First, if the President had wanted my help in fighting his father he would have asked for it.

Second, it's always stupid to get involved in a family scrap. In this case, it could be fatally stupid. The President wasn't a killer, I was certain. But there were those around him whose entire careers were based on killing.

And Wyatt—His Holiness: where did he stand? Which side was he on? Both? Neither? Wyatt could order a killing; I knew it in my bones. Under the proper circumstances he could commit murder himself.

Third, and most important, was the nagging doubt in my mind about the whole idea. If it was the General, why wouldn't the President simply drop a battalion of troops into Aspen and cart the old man off to a well-guarded rest home? Why all the pussyfooting? Why let the plot go on, and let good men like McMurtrie die? There was something more involved. Something I couldn't see. As yet.

I thought about calling Vickie to talk it over with her. But I decided against it. No sense getting her more involved than she was, either with the White House power struggle or with me, personally. *Never confuse a hard-on with love,* I warned myself. It was a motto that had saved me from many a pitfall. Ever since Laura.

So I ate my aluminum-wrapped dinner alone, drank the better part of a liter of Argentinian red, and trundled off to sleep on crisp clean sheets. Slept damned well, too, for a change.

Monday morning I got to the office a little earlier than usual. The lobby of the Aztec Temple was still mostly empty; the big rush crowd was a half-hour behind me. I took my usual elevator. Just as the doors started to close, another man stepped in, slipping sideways to avoid the rubber-edged doors.

"Close call," I said to him.

He nodded and mumbled something unintelligible.

I watched the numbers flicking by on the indicator lights. Halfway up to my floor, he said:

"You're Mr. Albano, aren't you? The Presidential press secretary?"

"That's right . . . Have we met?"

He shook his head as he extended his hand. I thought he wanted to shake hands, but instead he put a scrap of paper into my palm. I stared down at it. Penciled on it was: "Hogate's: 5:15 today."

As I looked up at the man again, he was punching the button for a floor below mine. "What in hell is this?" I asked him.

The elevator eased to a stop and the doors opened.

"Be there," he said as he stepped out.

The doors slid shut before I could say anything else. The elevator went on up to my floor. I got off, thinking to myself, *Now we're getting cloak-and-dagger dramatics.* I wondered if I should eat the note; that would be in style. Instead, I stuffed it into my shirtjac pocket and strode off to my office.

It was a busy morning. My picture-phone briefing with the President was spent going over the Kuwait situation and the upcoming reorganization of the State Department. So the press corps, when I gave them the morning rundown, spent damned near an hour asking about the Neo-Luddites and their impending march on Washington. Lazar's peace mission to Detroit had flopped, and for the moment the Middle East was pushed into the background.

Right after that I hustled over to the Oval Office for a face-to-face planning session about the President's upcoming press conference, which was due that Wednesday evening.

The Man was in his charming mood, relaxed, bantering with Wyatt and Frank Robinson, one of his speechwriters. We worked out an opening statement, dealing mainly with the new tax proposals he hoped to get through Congress before the summer recess. Since the package included cuts in personal income taxes, there were damned few Congressmen who'd take a strong stand against it. But since it also included selected increases in some corporate taxes, we knew they'd try to amend it to death. The President wanted to use his Wednesday press conference as a forum to forestall that kind of maneuvering.

"Go straight to the people," The Man told us. "Tell them what you want to do, openly and honestly. They'll recognize what's good for them and lean on their Congresspersons to get the job done. It's the President's task to get the people to think of the nation as a whole, instead of their own individual little interests. That's what we've got to do with every public utterance we make."

I glanced over at Wyatt. *Go straight to the people,* I thought. *But not about everything.* His Holiness looked right through me. As usual.

I was late for my monthly lunch with the Washington press corps. It was at the Van Trayer Hotel, on the site of the old Griffith Stadium in the northeast section of the District. People had called it "Van Trayer's Folly" when he built the hotel and shopping complex in the heart of the burned-out ghetto a dozen years earlier. But with Government help, that whole section of town was reborn and blossomed into an interracial, moderate-to-high-income community within the city. Very nice residential area now. The ghetto slums hadn't disappeared, of course; they'd just moved downtown, to the old shopping and theater areas.

Len Ryan was at the luncheon, a guest of one of the Washington TV stations. *He must be job hunting,* I thought. I got a lot of good-natured twitting about not being able to keep track of my boss's whereabouts, but most of the news people seemed happy enough that I was able to alert them, or their editors, about The Man's last-minute switch in plans before they trekked out to the wilds of Maryland.

I had to introduce the main speaker, a florid-faced

publisher from the West Coast who had started his meteoric rise to riches with the first three-dimensional girlie magazine and now was an outspoken champion of "freedom of the press" and the "right of free expression." The Supreme Court was reviewing his case; the state of Utah had tried to lock him up for pornography.

Ryan and I shared my official car back to the office, laughing at the guy's speech all the way. But once we got into my office and he unlimbered his tape recorder and Greta brought in a couple of frosty beers, Ryan got serious.

"I ought to be sore at you," he said, making something of a youthful scowl.

"Why? What'd I do?"

"I went down to Camp David Saturday, on my way down here . . ."

"Oh, crap, I didn't know. We alerted your paper's local office . . ."

Ryan took a long pull of his beer, and I watched his Adam's apple bob up and down.

"Doesn't matter," he said, thumping the half-empty mug on my desk. "The thing that bugs me is that you gave everybody the wrong poop."

I blinked. "Say again?"

"You put out the word that the President was staying in the White House all weekend. But he was actually having a secret conference in Camp David with the top Pentagon brass."

"Don't kid me, son," I said. But my stomach was starting to feel hollow. "You couldn't get close enough to see him if he was there, and he wasn't there in the first place."

"Wrong on both counts." Ryan leaned over and delved into the quarter-ton leather carrysack that he had brought with him. Out came a camera with a foot-long lens attachment.

"Electronic booster," he said. "Japanese. I could get close-ups of guys walking on the moon with this."

I tried to hide behind my beer mug.

"I figured something screwy was going on when the guards wouldn't even let me turn off the road," Ryan said, with a smug smile on his face. "They told me the President wasn't there—"

"He wasn't."

"But the word before I'd left Boston was that he'd be at Camp David all weekend."

"He changed his mind at the last minute."

"Yeah? Well, driving up to the camp, I saw enough helicopters—Army, mostly—to make it look like the place was being invaded."

My stomach lurched at that word.

Ryan was cheerfully oblivious to my distress. "Anyway, I figured something big was going on. So I drove a mile or so up the road, parked the car, and climbed a tree."

"Oh, for God's sake."

"Couldn't see much, but I got this one shot . . ." He pulled a three-by-five photograph from his pocket. Black and white. Handed it to me.

It was fuzzy, but it showed four men duck-walking out from under an Army helicopter's whirling rotors. Off to one side of the picture, three other men were standing waiting for them. The tallest one looked a helluva lot like James J. Halliday.

"Can't really see his face," I muttered.

"Yeah," said Ryan. "But you can see the stars on those generals' shoulders. And when they came up to that man they saluted him, like he was the Commander-in-Chief."

I shook my head, but without much enthusiasm. "That doesn't prove anything."

"Maybe, maybe not."

"What time was this taken?"

"Saturday . . . around six-thirty, seven o'clock."

This time I felt as if I were dropping down a chute. "I had dinner with the President at seven Saturday evening. In the White House," I said as evenly as I could. "He couldn't have been at Camp David when you took this photo." *He couldn't have been. But an-*

other double could. A double who was meeting with a lot of military brass, secretly, while the President argued with Admiral Del Bello.

Ryan grinned at me skeptically. "Okay. Go ahead and cover for your boss. It's part of the game. I expect it."

"Let's drop the subject," I said. "I'm telling you the truth and you don't believe it, so let's just drop it here and now."

"Okay by me," he answered. But the smug smile remained. It was a smile that said, *See, I'm still pure and holy, but you've sold out to the Establishment, and now you tell us lies.*

The thing that really pissed me off was that he was right, but in a way he didn't understand. I realized that I couldn't tell him what I knew, couldn't break the story to him. He probably wouldn't believe it. But he'd report it quickly enough. Oh sure, he'd report it. And inside of ten minutes I'd be wrapped in a plastic cocoon and on my way to the most remote funny farm in the land. And Ryan would be laughing about how guys crack up when they go to work for the Establishment.

I couldn't break this story with nothing to go on but my unsupported word. It would never get off the ground. Even if it got into the headlines, there'd be an official investigation, a whitewash, and the guy who originally spilled the story would quietly drop out of sight. I'd end up in an alcoholic ward somewhere, or maybe dead of an overdose of truth.

Not for me. Not yet, anyway. Not until I learned just what in hell was really going on.

So Ryan and I fenced our way through an interview, pinking each other here and there about the need for honesty from the President and his staff, and the need for responsibility from the news reporters. By the time he left, I was sore at him, more scared than ever, and even angrier at myself for what I had to do next.

I called Johnny Harrison in Boston and told him about Ryan's photograph.

"The kid's a little overeager, isn't he?" Harrison smiled slyly at me.

I grinned back into the phone screen. "He could get himself into trouble pulling stunts like that. Those laser-directed intruder alarms don't recognize press passes."

"Martyred reporters are good copy," Johnny said.

What about martyred editors? I wanted to ask. Instead, I said, "When you see that photograph, give me a call and tell me what you think of it."

"I've already seen it," he said. "Len sent a wire copy of it to me Saturday night. Interrupted my dinner with it."

"Well? What do you think?"

He shrugged. "Tempest in a teapot. I can't swear that it's the President in that picture, and neither can he. You say The Man was in the White House. Ryan says he's sneaking around with generals. Maybe. But that picture doesn't prove anything."

"There's nothing to prove," I insisted.

"Sure." But his face did a Groucho Marx version of, *If I believed that, I'd be as dumb as Harpo.*

"Well," I said weakly, "I just wanted to know what you planned to do."

He lifted his eyebrows. "Don't worry about that photo. But, ahhh, I *am* going to keep Ryan down in Washington for a while. Beef up our Washington bureau. And keep him out of my hair."

"Thanks a helluva lot," I said.

"All in a day's work," he answered cheerfully.

I damn near decided not to go to Hogate's that afternoon. I couldn't decide whether my elevator rendezvous was a joke, a serious attempt to recruit me for something secret, or a step in setting me up for the same kind of treatment McMurtrie had got.

But I went. Cursing myself for a damned fool, I went without telling anybody a word about it.

Hogate's had been a landmark in Washington for more than a century. The restaurant had gone through several incarnations, including being burned to the ground by insurgents once, during the battles of the late seventies. The newest Hogate's showed nothing more aboveground than a fair-sized plastic bubble. It was built down at the foot of Eleventh Street, right by the river. Most of the restaurant was subsurface. Not underground, but underwater: very fitting for a seafood restaurant.

It was like going to have a drink with Captain Nemo. You walked down a long, dank, tubular corridor, guided by faintly fluorescent patches of color arranged to look like moss or algae. The air was spiced with a salt tang, and a faint murmur of distant surf. A live mermaid with a plastic tail smiled at you through a heavy-looking hatch and you stepped into an aquarium. You're on the inside; the fish are on the outside, all around you. Fantastic effect with the shimmering light from the water and big toothy sharks sliding by six inches from your nose.

The main dining area was actually built like the interior of Nemo's Victorian submarine, complete with bookcases, pipe organ, and portholes that looked out on the ever-present fish.

I stood blinking in the dim light, trying to locate my taciturn contact man. I didn't remember much of what he looked like, and I didn't see anyone who seemed to be searching for me. So I sat at the bar and ordered a synthetic rum collins. The synthetics were pretty good; they tasted right and even got you high, but without the aftereffects. The FDA was investigating claims that they were addictive and carcinogenic. Considering what was boiling in my mind, I couldn't have cared less.

I was just coming to the conclusion that it was all a false alarm, when a lanky young man with longish sandy hair and a sad hound's face pulled up the stool next to mine.

"Mr. Albano," he said, without even looking at me.

THE MULTIPLE MAN 113

"That's my name. What's yours?"

"Hank Solomon."

"Hank . . . Solomon?"

"Don't especially care for people callin' me Sol. Or Henry." His voice had the dry drawl of the Southwest: Texas or Oklahoma.

The bartender was dressed like an old-time tar, with striped T-shirt and buttoned pants. Solomon ordered a straight bourbon and said nothing until the computer-operated mixing machine produced his drink and the bartender placed it in front of him.

"Good t'meet yew, Mr. Albano," said Hank Solomon.

"Thanks." I raised my glass to him.

"McMurtrie said yew were one of th' good people around th' President."

I felt my eyebrows hike up. "You knew McMurtrie?"

"Worked for him. I was one o' his outside boys. Naw, yew never saw me. I was always up ahead, makin' sure the President's path was cleared."

I nodded.

"Got a problem," he said. He was talking to me, but his eyes kept searching the room, going from the fairly well lit area of the bar out toward the dimmer sections of the restaurant and back again, ceaselessly.

"Something I can help you with?"

"Hope so." Solomon took a small, flat black box from his inside jacket pocket. It nestled easily in the palm of his hand. "Put this in yore shirt pocket and press this li'l button on top."

I did. Nothing happened.

Solomon glanced around the bar again, then added, "Now reach down alongside th' button and feel th' catch . . ." It was like a tiny metal hook. I could feel it with my fingernail. "Pull it loose and unreel th' earphone."

Now I got it. I gripped the tiny earphone between my forefinger and thumb and brought it up to my ear. It was a plug that fitted into my ear snugly.

". . . until further evidence is accumulated. End of report." It was McMurtrie's rumbling voice. I looked at Solomon; he sipped his bourbon and kept scanning the area. *What's he looking for?* I knew, in the abstract. But maybe he knew specifically what he was afraid of. McMurtrie's voice, a tiny pale ghost of his real voice, continued whispering in my ear. He gave the day and date and said:

"Progress report number six. Subject: investigation of possible Presidential assassination plot. Trip to North Lake Research Laboratories. Visited Dr. Alfonso Peña, head of lab. Also spoke with Dr. Peter Thornton and Dr. Morris Malachi. Was accompanied by Dr. Adrian Klienerman.

"Peña reports both Presidential doubles died of cause unknown. No violence. No poison. Klienerman checked Peña's test data but was not allowed to check the actual corpses. Nasty argument between Peña and Klienerman. Peña passed out. Thornton claimed it was heart trouble. He suggested that we get permission to let Klienerman do his own tests from General Halliday, who is the majority owner of North Lake Labs. Have booked flight to Aspen for Klienerman and myself to see the General."

My eyes focused on Solomon, the bar, the shadowy flickering underwater lighting beyond. But before I could say anything, McMurtrie's voice came on again.

"Additional note. Klienerman says duplicates could not possibly be so exactly similar to the President without, quote, biogenetic mapping, unquote. Then he said something about a band of brothers, or brotherhood. He was dozing as he said this, and is sleeping now, as we fly to Aspen. More later. Action item: get full background on Peña and North Lake Labs."

The spool stopped with a sharp click. I pulled the plug out of my ear and let the wire whiz back into the tape player in my shirt pocket.

Solomon had almost finished his drink. "That spool was mailed to the office from the Aspen airport, when Mac first landed there, on his way to see the General.

He addressed it to himself. Standard operatin' procedure."

I grabbed at my drink, suddenly wishing it were real rum. It took only one swallow to finish it.

"So what's your problem?" I asked as I put the glass back on the bar.

Solomon nodded to the bartender and kept silent until the refills were in front of us. "My problem's kinda simple. And kinda complicated. Nobody in the office is followin' up on Mac's reports."

"What?"

"I got th' tapes and papers and his ... well, what they call his 'effects.' I got assigned to sortin' 'em out and sendin' his personal stuff back to his wife ... er, widow."

"I never knew McMurtrie was married."

"Got two boys. One in college, th' other in the Aerospace Force. His wife lives in California."

"Hell," I said.

"Anyways, these progress reports on Mac's incomplete investigation sounded damned important to me. I took 'em to our section chief. He comes back a day later and says t' forget 'em. Bein' handled higher up."

"By whom?"

"By nobody, it turns out. Took me a coupla days of sniffin' around to find out. All Mac's reports were just tucked away in a file, locked up tight. And everybody in th' office is stonewallin' it. Mac's dead an' nobody's movin' an inch toward finishin' the investigation he was workin' on."

"They wouldn't do that without orders from higher up," I said.

"Yeah. I figured. But when this here tape arrived in th' mail yesterday, I got aholt of it before anybody else. Just luck. I was in the office early, when the first mail delivery come in."

"And the good old fucking mail service took a damned week to deliver his tape," I said.

Solomon broke into a lopsided grin. "Yeah."

"So you kept the tape?"

"Hell, no! Everything's logged in and double-checked in the office. I jest borrowed it for a few minutes and made my own copy of it ... before any-body else got into the office. I let the section chief have the tape soon's he showed up ... right 'bout time for the mornin' coffee break."

"And what was his reaction?" I asked.

"Combination scared and sore. I made sure he played the original tape while I was in the office. I volunteered t' take on Mac's action items an' check out that doctor and his lab. Chief said no. Buck it up-stairs."

"And you think it's being buried."

His smile disappeared. "I know it's buried. This in-vestigation's as dead as Mac, far's the office's con-cerned. That's why I looked you up. Mac tole me once you could be trusted."

"I'm just a glorified public relations man ..."

"Yew work right for th' President," Solomon said. "I don't know anybody in th' Government's any higher ... that I can trust."

I caught myself in the middle of taking a very deep breath, the kind that steadies your pulse rate. Or so they say.

"Okay," I said. "I don't know what the hell I'm going to do about this, but I'll do something. It sure looks as if Klienerman was killed because he was catching onto something important."

"And Mac along with him."

"Right." I could feel my jaw clenching. "I don't suppose anybody's actually checked out this man Peña and the North Lake Labs."

"Nope. But I can get that done."

"Really? When I tried it—"

"Mac had a lotta friends. In the Pentagon, too. We can find out what we have to know. Might take a few days, is all."

"Good. Now, should I keep this tape or should you?"

"Me," he said, holding out his hand. "They already

know I'm sniffin' around on this. Less they know about yew bein' involved, better off we both'll be."

I handed the palm-sized black box back to him. "Hank . . . do you have any idea of who *they* are?"

He shook his head. "Wish I did."

"It's like staggering around in the dark, isn't it?"

"Yep. One thing, though . . ."

"What's that?"

"The President's ol' man is involved, some way."

It was a while before I could answer. "Yeah . . . I think you're right."

"Helluva world, ain't it?" he said, and grabbed his bourbon.

CHAPTER ELEVEN

Most people think that the National Archives is the nation's treasure house of information, the memory storage bin of the country, the place where all the facts are kept neatly filed away behind a facade that proclaims, "What is past is prologue."

But we were meeting at the Library of Congress—Vickie, Hank Solomon, and I—sneaking into that vast marble-walled building from three different entrances, at three different times, in a feeble effort to prevent anyone from figuring out that we were getting together there. It was Vickie's idea to pick the Library of Congress, and Hank's to stagger our arrival times. I did what I was told.

Hank's friends had been able to piece together a lot more information about Dr. Peña and his lab than Vickie had. But it was still damned sketchy.

According to FBI and Defense Department records, Dr. Alfonso Peña had been working in biological warfare studies almost all his life. Never mind that biowar research was officially renounced by all the major nations more than a generation ago. Never mind that a treaty signed by the U.S. and ratified by the Senate has the force of law, and thus any research banned by treaty is actually illegal within the United States.

Peña had started as a brilliant, promising young biochemist more than half a century ago, accepted a position at the old Army Chemical Warfare center in Edgewood, Maryland, straight out of college. Then he transferred to Fort Detrick and biological warfare studies: how to use disease as a weapon of war. When Fort Detrick was officially "peacified" and turned into a cancer research center, Peña went right along without changing his line of research in the slightest. By then he was deeply into genetic research, tinkering with the basic chemical of life, the long double-helix molecules that the bio people call DNA.

Not even Solomon's friends could trace Peña's career year by year. But shortly after North Lake Labs changed owners—it had started as a dairy research adjunct to the University of Minnesota—Peña showed up there as its new director. The new owner of North Lake Labs? A consortium of businessmen whom I'd never heard of before: small-timers, all of them. Except for the majority owner: Morton J. Halliday, who at that time was neither a general nor a national hero.

North Lake prospered mainly through contracts with the Defense Department. Most of the work was so deeply classified that *nobody* outside the direct chain-of-command could get an eye on it.

But Solomon got something that might have been almost as good: a personnel roster of the research staff of North Lake, a roster that went back to the labs' change of ownership some forty-three years earlier. It was a long list, and Solomon had no way of knowing if it was complete. But it was all we had to go on.

It was evening when I showed up at the Library of Congress, and yet the building was still busy with people. I had always pictured the Library as a musty old place, quiet and slumbering, disturbed only by an occasional Senator who needed a place to get away from his constituents. But the Library was alive, mostly with young people who were eagerly tapping the nation's storehouse of books, films, tapes, knowledge. Everything and anything was on tap in the Library's computerized memory files. *This* was the real information center of the nation.

It took me damned near an hour to find Vickie

inside that building. She had told me the number of the room she had reserved under her own name. But I was reluctant to go blundering through the place asking questions, leaving a trail that could be followed blindfolded.

So I wandered through the high-ceilinged reading rooms, marble hallways that echoed my footfalls, long rows of reading booths where video screens flickered with page after page of the nation's treasure house of books while intent young students or Congressional aides studied and copied down notes, somber-faced and greenish in the light from the electronic screens.

I even wandered into the computer center, down in the first subbasement, by mistake. The machine was so damned vast that I couldn't see the end of it; just bank after bank of man-tall consoles humming and blinking, right on down an entire level of the Library's underground labyrinth.

No one was there except a pleasant-looking young woman who looked up from her control desk and saw me standing there, gawking stupidly under the glareless ceiling light panels that seemed to stretch off to infinity. She got up from her desk and walked over to me. She was wearing jeans and a pullover sweater; it was quite cool down there. With a no-nonsense smile she asked me where I was going. I tried to sound like a bewildered Midwestern tourist and succeeded only in sounding bewildered. I gave her a room number on a different level and she gave me polite instructions. She punched the wall button behind me, the elevator door slid open, and she bade me a polite but firm good-by. She was very protective of that mammoth computer.

I finally found Vickie, and Hank was already with her. The room was only one level above the computer area, still underground and windowless. It was a small reading room, furnished with two chairs and a picture screen sitting on a tiny desk, soundproofed in that funny airless way that makes it feel as if somebody's holding his hands over your ears.

Hank started to get up and offer me his seat, but I

told him to stay where he was. I'd been sitting all damned day; it felt good to give my butt a rest. But the room *was* small, too small for three people, and as I leaned my shoulder against the thin plywood of the door I felt just the slightest bit trapped, claustrophobic.

"Okay, Vickie," I said, trying to override my inner tension, "this is your show. What'd you call us here for?"

She was wearing a miniskirt and a loose blouse, open at the throat. Hank had already taken a more than professional interest in keeping an eye on her. He had doffed his "business" suit in favor of a faded denim jacket and corduroy slacks—made him look more like an unkempt perennial student than a Secret Service agent. Except for his hair, which was too long for a modern student's. He was even smoking. Synthetic tobacco, from the perfumy smell of it. Noncarcinogenic, according to the corporate advertising claims. The air conditioning sucked the smoke up into a ceiling vent.

Vickie tapped the computer read-out screen with a fingernail. "We've all been trying to get information together about Dr. Peña and North Lake Labs . . ."

"Maybe we oughtta put General Halliday on our list," Hank suggested. "Him and those friends o' his that helped him buy North Lake."

"I've already done that," Vickie said, very professionally competent. "I took their biographies from a *Who's Who* and other references before you two showed up."

"Okay, so we've got a pile of biographical information," I said. "I don't see how that helps us to find out who's doing what to whom. And *that's* our real goal."

"Our first goal," Hank said, squinting narrow-eyed at me, past the cigarette smoke, "our real objective, is t' set things straight after we find out who's doin' what."

"If we can," I said.

He nodded grimly, and I caught a mental flash of Hank gunning down, Western style with blazing revolvers, whoever had killed McMurtrie. It was a personal matter with him.

Vickie resumed. "We have access to an enormous amount of information here. This computer can tell us almost anything—"

"Except what we want to know," I said.

"Wrong." She had a very serious look on her face, but there was something else going on behind those sea-green eyes. She was excited, anticipating.

"Wrong?" I echoed.

"Wrong," she confirmed. "This computer can do something more for us. It can correlate all the information we have, find the connections, pull out the key links for us . . ."

Hank was skeptical. "You mean a *computer* can go through a pile of information and find out what's important to us and toss away th' rest? Like a human detective?"

"Not quite," Vickie said, "but close enough. See, this is a specialized computer. It's programmed to serve the needs of the people who use the Library of Congress. People come here with a few scraps of information and ask the computer for help in finding more, just as they'd ask a librarian."

"And yore sayin' that a librarian works like a detective?" Hank didn't believe a word of it.

Vickie answered, "Sort of. You give a librarian a few clues and she'll usually be able to find what you're looking for. This computer," she tapped the screen again, "will do the same thing. Only better, faster, and with a much bigger memory than any human librarian has."

Hank just shook his head.

I said, "So you're saying that if we feed the computer all the information we have, it can point out the connections—"

"That's right," Vickie answered, bobbing her head

vigorously enough to make her golden hair jounce prettily.

"I'm not sure . . ."

"You're an ex-newspaper reporter," Vickie said to me. "Your method of getting information is to grab people by the neck and fire questions at them. I'm a researcher. I find information by going through records, dealing with computers and librarians and reference books. Your way hasn't produced very much, boss. Not yet, anyway. I want to try my method."

"With an electronic detective," Hank added, still skeptical.

I shrugged at her. "Okay. Let's see what you get."

She started with the biographical information from General Halliday and the others who had purchased North Lake Labs more than forty years ago. Vickie typed on the computer's input keyboard a request for correlations among the biographies of the nine men involved; in other words, how they were linked. The computer's output screen showed the shorthand words she typed:

RE INPUT CODE 042205-B219-001
REQ CORR SCH

Her words glowed green on the picture tube for a few moments while the computer considered the problem. Then a list of the nine names flashed, so briefly that I'm not sure all nine of them were there. Then the screen filled with words, pica-sized green letters covering the whole screen, from top to bottom, side to side. And at the very last was a word in parentheses that I instantly recognized: (MORE). This one screenful of data wasn't all that the computer had dug up.

We got very excited, but quickly found that the correlations were nothing more than we would have expected. Four of the nine co-owners of North Lake Labs had worked for General Halliday at one time or another. Two more were relatives of the General's, distant cousins. The remaining two men were real estate executives in Minnesota: the front men who did the actual buying.

Of the nine original buyers, only three were still alive: the General, of course; one of the real estate operators, who now lived in Sri Lanka; and the only woman in the deal, who had been the General's secretary back when he had served in the Pentagon as a major in the Army Research Office. The computer had no information on her whereabouts.

"Not much goddamned help," Hank muttered.

"No," I agreed. "Except that I get the feeling that all the money involved came from the General himself. These other eight people were just strawmen, dummies to cover up the General's intention to own the Labs himself. And control them."

"Where'd he get that kind of money?" Vickie asked. "He couldn't have been more than thirty years old or so at the time."

The biographical data didn't tell us much. General Halliday had been thirty-two when the North Lake Labs were sold to his group. He had been working in the Pentagon at that time. His hero-making defense of Denver was still nearly ten years in the future. He had married a fairly wealthy Virginia socialite, but as yet they had no children.

"Maybe his wife put up the money," I said.

"More likely she put up th' collateral for a bank t' loan him th' money," Hank said. "Musta been at least ten million involved. Prob'ly more."

I thought aloud, "The Government was phasing down research funding then. Lots of economic scares, the whole Vietnam fiasco and the turbulence of the sixties and seventies. Universities were pulling in their horns; money was tight, especially in scientific research . . ."

"But suppose a bright, ambitious young Army officer who worked in the Pentagon . . ." Vickie mused.

"In the Army Research Office," I added.

"Suppose he went to a bank."

Hank chimed in, "Or a dinner party full of bankers, set up by his purty young wife . . ."

I took over again, "And offered them a scheme where he attains a controlling interest in a research laboratory, which he can set up so that it can be guaranteed a steady flow of Army research money . . ."

"The bank would get its loan repaid in a few years," Vickie said.

"At the highest interest rates of the century. And Halliday retires from the Army after the loan is paid off and goes to live in Colorado . . ."

"Where he continues to pull the strings . . ."

"And becomes a rich son of a bitch."

We looked at one another. We were grinning and nodding excitedly. Proud of our terrific powers of deduction.

Hank broke the bubble. "But what in hell's all this got t' do with th' President? He wasn't even born yet!"

We went back to being gloomy. Hank produced his thick wad of biographical information about the labs' research staff scientists. With a resigned sigh, Vickie began typing the information into the computer. Most of the data had come from standard reference sources such as *American Men and Women of Science,* so Vickie could simply cite the reference, and the computer would know where to look. Still, it was a long job.

I ducked out to the men's room and then volunteered to take over the typing. "Just tell me what to do," I said.

Vickie argued at first, but finally relented and let me hammer the keys while she worked the kinks out of her hands. Hank disappeared briefly and came back with sandwiches and coffee.

"How long's this place stay open?" I wondered.

" 'Til ten," Hank said. "I just checked."

"We've only got—"

"We've got as long as we need," Vickie said. "I commandeered this room for Senator Markley. Senators and Congresspersons and their staffs can stay all night, if they want to. The computer's on-line twenty-four hours a day, seven days a week."

"Wonderful," I heard myself say.

We took a brief dinner break, wolfing the sandwiches and coffee, and then Vickie took over the input typing again.

"Should've brought some beer," I said to Hank.

"Didn't even think of it," he admitted, looking surprised at himself.

Finally the job was done. All the biographical data about every researcher we knew had worked at North Lake was in the computer's memory bank. Vickie punched the request to correlate the data, and while the computer chewed on the problem, she stood up, put her arms over her head and stretched hard enough to pop tendons along her spine. It was a move that stirred my blood, and I could see that it did the same for Hank. Vickie didn't seem to notice, though. Or care.

"How long d'yew think it'll take th' machine to figure things out?"

Vickie shrugged. "A few minutes, maybe. That's a lot of data to cross-correlate."

"You really think this will give us an insight on what's going on at North Lake?" I asked her.

"It will at least tell us the common denominators among the scientific staff there. If it turns out that they're all specialists in building hydrogen bombs, for example, do you think the labs' main interest would be in air pollution studies?"

"Nobody likes a wiseass," I said.

Vickie grinned and started to rub the back of her neck. Hank was over behind her like a shot, kneading her shoulders.

"Learned massage from an ol' Indian," he drawled. Vickie moaned happily and I broiled medium-rare.

The computer screen came to life. A list of words appeared on it. A damned short list. We all huddled around the glowing screen, like kids peeking into a store window. The list read:

MAJOR FIELDS OF COMMON INTEREST
INPUT CODE 042205-B219-004

ORGANIC CHEMISTRY	INFECTIOUS DISEASES
BIOCHEMISTRY	VIRAL BIOLOGY
GENETICS	IMMUNOLOGY
MOLECULAR BIOLOGY	BEHAVIORAL PSYCHOLOGY

INFORMATION THEORY

We stared at the list for a long time. At last Hank exploded, "That don't tell us diddley-shit!"

"Wait a minute," Vickie said. She sat at the keyboard again and tapped out a query, explaining as she typed the cryptic shorthand words, "I'm asking what kinds of capabilities these fields of interest could produce."

The machine considered this problem for only a few seconds, then flashed a new list on the screen. It was a lot longer, and full of technical terms that I'd never seen before. But three items stuck out and hit me just as if they'd been printed in letters of fire:

BIOLOGICAL WARFARE
GENETIC ENGINEERING
CLONING

CHAPTER TWELVE

Before either of the others could say anything, I told Vickie, "Ask the computer for a definition of cloning."

She looked up at me quizzically, but her fingers tapped out the query. The computer screen immediately showed:

CLONE: The descendants produced vegetatively or by apomixis from a single plant; asexually or by parthenogenesis from a single animal; by division from a single cell. The members of a clone are of the same genetic constitution, except insofar as mutation occurs amongst them.

"That's it," I said. "Somebody's made clone copies of the President."

"Hey now, slow down a minute fer us ol' country boys," Hank said. "What're yew—"

Vickie explained, "Scientists can take a cell from your body . . . any cell, like from your skin or a fingernail clipping, and reproduce exact copies of you from it. The babies grown from your cells would turn out to look exactly like you. You could make as many copies of yourself as you want, that way."

"Exact duplicates," I said. "As many as you want."

Hank wasn't as slow as he liked to pretend. "Y'all mean I could make a roomful of copies of *me?*"

"Right."

"Without sex? Just by takin' a few cells off the end o' my nose or somethin'?"

I nodded.

"Sheeit. . . . First place, I don't *want* more copies o' me runnin' around. Second place, I like the old way of makin' babies a helluva lot better."

Vickie was grinning at him, but I said, "It's obvious that somebody wants a lot of copies of the President running around."

"But nobody's cloned human beings," Vickie said. "That whole line of research was shut down years and years ago. The biologists themselves stopped the experiments."

"Nobody's *reported* cloning human beings," I shot back, jerking a thumb at the computer screen. "But the capability's there."

Hank asked slowly, "Y'all think somebody's taken some cells from th' President's body . . . and grown extra people from them? People who look jest like th' President?"

"That can't be," Vickie objected before I could answer. "It would still take forty-some years to grow those cells to the same level of maturity as the President."

It was all clicking into place in my mind. I asked Vickie, "How much do you want to bet that the biologists outlawed human cloning experiments right around the time the General brought out North Lake Labs?"

She stared at me, speechless.

"James J. Halliday was cloned in infancy," I said, the words coming fast and eager, "and his father bought the North Lake Labs specifically for that purpose."

"When th' kid was born?"

Vickie said, *"Before* the child was born. General Halliday bought the labs before the President was born."

"He did it deliberately," I said. "He planned it all out some forty-five years ago!"

"We're seeing the results of a plan that's been in operation for nearly half a century." Vickie looked and sounded just as awed and frightened as I felt.

Hank tried to pull us back to reality. "But *why?* Why th' hell would he want t' make extra copies of his own son? And what's happenin' to those copies now?"

I had no answer. Yet. "All right, let's put together the pieces we have and see if any of this really makes sense," I said.

They both waited for me to say more. I leaned my rump against the edge of the desk and started ticking off points on my fingers.

"One: when the President's father was a major in the Army Research Office, he pulled a deal that got him major ownership and complete control of the North Lake Research Laboratories."

They both nodded.

"Two: he brings Dr. Alfonso Peña in to head up North Lake. Peña had been working in biological warfare at Fort Detrick."

"Halliday prob'ly knew Peña already," Hank threw in.

I agreed with a nod. "Three: Halliday retires to Colorado and becomes filthy rich. He keeps a commission in the National Guard and becomes a big hero when Denver's threatened by food rioters."

"And in th' meantime he has a son," said Hank.

"Right. What about his wife?" I wondered.

"She died while the boy was still an infant," Vickie said. "I checked that out earlier. Natural causes, although there was some gossip in the underground press around Aspen that she drank herself to death."

"Okay," I said. "Now where the hell are we?"

"Point four."

I saw that my hands were trembling slightly. Nobody seemed to notice. "All right. Four: General Halliday had his son cloned at North Lake, either right at birth or very soon afterward. Vickie, is there any info on *where* the President was born?"

"At the General's home in Aspen."

"So he flew the kid to Minnesota right after birth?" Hank asked.

"Not necessarily," I said. "All they had to do was ship a few cells from the baby's body out to the labs. A little sliver of skin would do."

"Maybe when they circumcised him," Vickie suggested, a trace of a smile on her lips.

"How do you know he was circumcised?"

"I could try to find out."

"Never mind. They only needed a few cells. That would be enough to grow as many 'extra' James J. Hallidays as they wanted. Each of them only nine months or so younger than the original."

"It still don't make sense." Hank was shaking his head doggedly. "Why would th' General clone his son? How could they keep th' thing a secret? Cryin' out loud—they'd have a dozen little James J. Hallidays crawlin' all over th' place!"

"No wonder his mother drank herself to death," Vickie said. But there was no smile this time.

"The General's hideout at Aspen is big enough to stash a battalion of James J. Hallidays," I said.

"But the *secrecy* they'd need t' carry it off!" Hank insisted. "Why, th' General'd have to have a staff of people who looked up t' him like he was God, fer cryin' out loud."

I grinned humorlessly. "Ever meet the General?"

"Nope."

"Or some of his employees ... like Robert H. H. Wyatt?"

"Oh." Hank had met Wyatt, it was apparent. "Maybe I see what yew mean."

"Okay then ... putting it all together ..."

Vickie took over. "The General had his son cloned, and then trained him for a life in politics. He was *programmed* to be President from the instant he was born."

"Before that," I said.

"But why clone him?" Hank asked again. "And

why're th' clones droppin' dead? Who's killin' them? And why?"

"That's what we've got to find out," I said.

"How?"

"There's one guy who knows the whole story, and he might be pressured into telling us: Dr. Peña."

Vickie said, "McMurtrie and Dr. Klienerman talked with Peña just before they . . . they crashed."

"I know." That's why my hands were shaking, and why I belatedly looked up at the ventilator grill in the ceiling and started to wonder who else had heard our think-tank session.

CHAPTER THIRTEEN

General Halliday beat us to the punch.

I got into my office early the next morning and dove into the pile of accumulated paperwork that Greta had left on my desk—until 9:00 Central Time. Then I put in a call to Dr. Peña.

And got Peter Thornton. On the phone's picture screen, he looked even fussier and more officious than he had in person.

"Dr. Peña's not available," he said. "He's been under *enough* strain recently."

"This is important," I said. "I want to fly out there this afternoon and—"

"Absolutely not! Out of the question. Besides, he won't even be here by this afternoon. He's going away for a *complete* rest."

"Away? Where?"

Thornton's normally frowning face wrinkled even further into a scowl. "Oh, come now, Mr. Albano. Why can't you leave the old man alone? He's *very* frail, and quite upset about all this . . . this . . . notoriety."

I leaned closer to the phone screen. "Listen. Would you rather have him talk to me or to the Federal goddamned Bureau of Investigation?"

"Really! I—"

"Where's he going?" I demanded. "To the General's place in Aspen?"

Thornton looked shocked. "How did you know?"

"I've got spies, too."

"But . . ."

"I know," I said. "Dr. Peña needs a complete rest. You just make sure he doesn't get the kind of rest that Klienerman and McMurtrie got."

"What? What are you *saying?*"

"Nothing. Just take good care of that old man." I clicked off before he could say anything else.

And called Vickie into my office. In the few minutes it took to get her down the hall I signed half a dozen memos and canceled three meetings that I was supposed to chair.

Vickie came in quietly, without any announcement from Greta, and took the seat in front of my desk. She was wearing a forest-green one-piece jumpsuit, with a yellow scarf tied loosely at her throat.

"Looks like you're ready to go skydiving," I said as I initialed a couple more memos.

She grinned at me. "It's a comfortable outfit. I don't have any outside appointments today, so I can wear what feels best."

"Looks good," I said.

She made a *thank-you* bob of her head.

"I'm going to Aspen," I said. "The General's got Dr. Peña there."

Vickie's face went from pleased to surprised to scared to thoughtful, all in a couple of eyeblinks. She was terrible at keeping secrets.

"What good will that do?" she asked in a level, practicality-above-all tone. "The General probably won't even let you into his house, and even if he does, he certainly won't let you interrogate Dr. Peña."

"Can you think of anything better we can do?"

She pursed her lips for a moment. "Yes. Call a press conference and tell the newshawks what you know."

"Blow the lid off."

"Exactly." Her face was dead serious now.

"I can't do that, Vickie . . . not just yet, anyway. I promised The Man that I'd keep things buttoned up—"

"He can't hold you to such a promise!"

"Maybe not. But *I* can. I gave The Man my word, kid. I can't go back on that, not yet."

"When, for God's sake? After you're smashed all across some Colorado mountainside?"

"Don't get emotional."

"Don't get chauvinistic," she snapped back. "I'm a damned sight more practical than you, Meric. I don't let Boy Scout oaths straitjacket my thinking. You swore secrecy to the President! Is that worth your life? Or his?"

I tried to stay calm. Vickie seemed more angry than anything else. And she had some accurate thinking on her side.

"Listen ... Vickie ... when we go to the press, I want to be able to give them the whole story. Who, what, where, when, how. Right now, all we know is that the President was cloned in infancy, and at least two of the clones are dead of unknown causes."

"And McMurtrie and Klienerman were murdered."

"Maybe."

"They're certainly dead."

"Okay." I found myself drumming my fingertips on the desk top. I pulled back my hands and drummed on my thighs instead. Quieter, at least.

"If we release what we know to the press," I went on, "it will ruin the President. Just blow him right out of office. He'll be totally unable to do his job."

"Is that bad?"

"Do we know for sure that it's not?" I demanded, my voice rising. "Has he done anything to deserve being tossed out like a crook or an incompetent? Has he tried to squash us? He could, you know, in about twelve microseconds."

"Well ..."

"He's been doing a damned fine job, hasn't he?"

"Yes, but ..."

"Vickie, listen to me. We have absolutely no evidence that the President is involved in anything nefarious. For a while there I thought he was—but now, I'm not so sure. For all we know, he was never told about this cloning. It's the General who's behind all this. And it's our job to find out what the General's doing, and why, without harming the President."

"But suppose the President *is* part of it? Whatever it is," Vickie asked, leaning forward in her chair, earnest, intent, afraid.

"If we find out he's part of it, we blow the whistle. Loud and clear. But not until then."

She shook her head unhappily.

"I'm going to Aspen," I said. "I've got to see Dr. Peña, one way or the other."

"It's a trap," Vickie said. "They've been watching every move we make, and they're setting you up for the same treatment that McMurtrie got."

"That's . . . melodramatic," I said. Limply.

"They're using Peña as bait. They *want* you to go there."

"Okay," I said, trying to sound tough, "they're going to get their wish."

Vickie sat up straighter and looked at me with calm, serious eyes. "So you're going to march into the lion's den, and I'm supposed to stay safely at home and keep your obituary notice handy, in case it comes to that."

I had to smile at her. "I think I hear a feminist tirade coming at me."

"You're not leaving me behind," she said. "I'm not some simpering *hausfrau* . . ."

"No. But you *are* the person who can call an international press conference if anything happens to me. There's no sense *both* of us walking into the lion's den."

"Then let me go, and you stay here."

"Not on your life!"

A quizzical look came over her face. "That's an interesting choice of words."

"All right," I said. "The argument is closed. I'm going to Aspen this afternoon. You hold the fort here."

She didn't answer. It was impossible for that elfin face to sulk, but she was damned close to it.

"And I want you to stay with friends while I'm

away," I added. "You're not immune to an accident here in Washington, you know."

"I have some friends I could stay with," she said.

"Male or female?"

Vickie arched an eyebrow. "Does it make any difference?"

"Would I ask if it didn't?"

She smiled. But she didn't answer.

I took the United flight to Denver and the Rocky Mountain Airways bounce-along to Aspen. Deciding that boldness was my best protection, I rented a helicopter and told the pilot to land me at the pad alongside the General's house.

"I gotta have clearance first," he told me over the whine of the chopper's turbines. "Those guys don't think twice about shootin' at ya."

He was a grizzled, fiftyish, hulking bear of a man, the kind who didn't look as if he scared easily. On the other hand, a man doesn't earn a living flying in the tricky air currents of the Rockies if he's inclined to take chances and trust to luck.

We were already airborne and in five minutes we'd be over the General's estate.

"Okay," I said to the pilot. "You raise them on the radio, but let me talk to them."

He gave me a wary glance but did it anyway. I took a headset from his chunky hand as the valley slid below us. The chopper was riding fast and low; the air was smooth enough to make the ride almost pleasant. The snow was still heavy on the ground, broken only by plowed roads and the dark green of big fir trees reaching up toward us. The town was behind us, out of sight. The only signs of habitation I could see were occasional houses or ski lodges sitting low and stony against the snowy fields.

As I clamped the headset on, a tinny voice grated in my ear: "Who's asking for landing clearance? Repeat, who is requesting landing clearance?" The voice already sounded annoyed.

"This is Meric Albano, press secretary to the President of the United States." The title always impressed the hell out of me; maybe it would buffalo them a little. "We'll be landing in a red and white Snowbird Lines helicopter in about three or four minutes. I'm here to see General Halliday and Dr. Peña."

"I'll have to check with—"

"Check with whoever you want to, after I've landed. We're coming down and we don't want any interference. If there is any trouble, the President will hear about it immediately."

We landed without trouble. But it seemed to me that my pilot could've waited until I was clear of his rotor downwash before he took off again. He jerked that whirly-bird off the General's property like a spatter of grease jumping off a hot skillet.

I coughed the dust and grit out of my face and followed an escort of three very large men—the kind who go from careers in the state police to careers in private goon squads. They led me up to the house, but apparently they were strictly outside men. I was picked up at the door by a very polite Oriental, dressed more or less as a butler. Probably could crack bank vaults with a single chop of his hand.

The butler was extremely polite. He showed me into a very comfortable sitting room with a view of the valley through the ceiling-high windows. He spoke in a very soft voice, with an accent that was more UCLA than the other side of the Pacific. He asked me if I cared for anything to drink. I said no. He bowed slightly, just a slight inclination of his head.

"General Halliday was not expecting visitors this afternoon. He begs your indulgence for a few moments."

"I'll wait," I said.

"Is there anything I could do to make you more comfortable?"

"You could tell Dr. Peña that I'm here and want to talk with him."

He blinked. For a moment I got the impression that

he was a cleverly built transistorized robot, run by a computer that had to search through its entire instruction program to find the correct response to the mention of Dr. Peña's name.

At last he said, "I don't believe Dr. Peña is receiving any visitors at all."

"But he is here."

"So I have been told. I have not seen him myself."

I nodded. "Thanks."

He bowed, a little deeper this time, and withdrew from the room.

It was a large room, very pleasantly decorated. Rustic style. Knotty pine paneling. Big gnarled beams across the ceiling. Stone fireplace with a grizzly bear rug in front of it. Balcony outside the windows. I walked across a scattering of Navaho carpets and admired the view: the mountains were still glittering with snow, forests of pine and spruce marching up their flanks. I couldn't see the valley or the town from here. Maybe from the balcony. I tried the sliding glass doors. They were locked.

I spun around and saw that the room had only one other door, the one I had come in through. It was closed. I hurried across to try the handle. It was locked, too. I wasn't getting out of this room until the General wanted me out.

So I sat around and waited, trying not to get the shakes. There were no books to read. The fireplace was cold and dark. A few magazines were scattered on the coffee table in front of the room's only couch—old issues of *Camping Guide* and *Investor's Weekly*. I gave the phone a try and got that oh-so-polite Oriental butler, who informed me that General Halliday had requested that I refrain from making any outside calls until he had spoken with me.

In disgust, and to keep my mind from winding itself up into a terrified little knot, I turned on the television set and watched an idiotic children's show about a park ranger and his teenaged kids who somehow had gotten themselves mixed up with dinosaurs.

During the fourteenth breakfast food commercial, the General came in. I didn't hear the door open behind me, but the TV picture winked off. I turned and there he was, leaning over stiffly, one hand still on the control keyboard set into the little table next to the door.

"I'm glad to see that you found something to occupy your mind while you were waiting," he said as I got up from my chair. He was far from smiling.

"I'm glad to see you didn't keep me waiting all that long. Time passes slowly in jail." I decided as the words were coming out that I'd better not let him think he could cow me. Old reporter's habit: mouth first, then brain. Instinct followed by rationalization.

"Just what in hell are you trying to do, Albano?" The General normally looked annoyed at lesser creatures. Now he looked blazingly angry.

"I'm trying to save your son's life ... and his Presidency. Or doesn't that matter to you?"

He hadn't budged an inch from where I'd first seen him. "Get out of here," he said, his voice low and slightly trembling. "You wise-mouthed son of a bitch ... get out of my house!"

"Sure," I said, taking a couple of steps toward him and the door. "But once I'm outside I'm going to call a press conference and blast this story wide open."

"Like hell you will."

"If you're thinking I won't make it back to Washington, guess again. An assistant of mine knows all about this, and she'll take over if anything happens to me."

He didn't bat an eye. "If you mean Ms. Clark, forget it. She can be bought off very easily. Or silenced."

Jesus! "Maybe so," I bluffed. "But I've also spilled the story to a reporter who'll break it as soon as anything happens to either one of us."

"And who might that be?"

"You'll find out if you try to hurt Vickie ... or me."

"Ryan? That young pup from Boston?"

"It doesn't make any difference. We've got this thing fail-safed. You can't hurt us."

He stamped into the room, right past me and over to the windows. I could see the cords in his scrawny old neck popping out. His fists clenched.

"Why?" He whirled around to face me again. "Who's backing you, Albano? Who's behind you?"

I should have tried eloquence and said, *The people of the United States of America.* Instead I answered, "Nobody. Except the President."

"Cut the crap."

"I mean it! Somebody's out to get the President—your son. Either to kill him or discredit him so completely that he'll be forced to resign."

The General shook his head.

"And whoever's doing this, he's operating from right here. I think it's you, or somebody working for you."

"You're dead wrong," he said quietly, without fire.

"We know about the cloning," I said.

His face went white.

"We know that Dr. Peña did it. And we know that he's here. That's who I came to see. I want to find out what he knows about all this. And I want to hear what you've got to say. You've got at least two murders on your doorstep ..."

"Murders?"

"McMurtrie and Dr. Klienerman."

"That was an accident!"

"The hell it was!"

"It was, dammit!" he shouted. But standing there by the windows, with the fading afternoon sun at his back, he somehow looked weaker, less certain of himself, starting to bend.

I pushed harder. "McMurtrie and Klienerman were killed after they talked with Peña and he sent them here. Two cloned duplicates of the President were killed . . ."

"No . . ."

"Goddammit, stop lying to me!" I exploded. "Stop this motherfucking phony shit or I'll go right out of here and tear your son's Presidency apart! Is that what you want? Is that what you're after?"

For a long moment he didn't answer. Didn't move. Just stood there with his hands hanging loosely at his sides, looking old and uncertain. He shook his head and mumbled something too low for me to hear. Then he walked slowly to the phone, pressed the ON stud, and said softly:

"Ask Dr. Peña if he feels up to joining us here in the first floor sitting room."

I let my breath out in a long, slow sigh.

The General looked up from the phone, his face more sad than angry. "Don't think you've won anything, wise mouth. And don't think you *know* anything."

"And don't think I can be conned," I replied.

He seemed to regain a little of his strength. "Sit down. I'll order some drinks. You've got a lot to learn, Mr. Press Secretary. A hell of a lot."

The Oriental brought a tray of decanters and glasses and bowed his way out of the room again, all without making a discernible sound. When I hesitated at accepting anything, the General laughed at me, not without some bitterness.

"Stop playing cloak and dagger. I'm not going to poison you, for Christ's sake."

I picked up one of the glasses and poured from the same decanter the General did. Took ice from the same bucket with the same tongs. It was straight rye; not my favorite, but he was drinking it, so I sipped at mine.

He leaned back in one of the deep leather chairs. "You know about the cloning, then."

"Yes . . . and the fact that two of the clones have been killed."

"They're dead," he insisted. "That doesn't mean they were murdered."

"Peña can prove it, if he wants to."

"Don't be too sure."

At that moment, the door opened again and Dr. Peña wheeled into the room. He did look even more frail and drawn than when I'd seen him ten days ago. His face was sinking in on itself, cheeks hollow and eyes cavernous pits so deep you couldn't see any spark of life in them. The skin on his hands seemed paper thin, so that every tendon and blood vessel stood out like a drawing in a medical textbook. He was wearing an oversized caftan, although for all I know it might have fitted him perfectly at one time. The robe bulked oddly, showing the outlines of the equipment that was fastened to his body.

The General shot me a black look as Dr. Peña wheeled his chair slowly toward us. He was saying, *See? You've come to persecute a dying man.*

God help me, I had just the opposite reaction. I wanted to pump his information out of him before he dropped dead.

"You asked me to join you," Dr. Peña said to the General. It was a flat statement, neither questioning nor accusatory. His voice was a bare whisper, nothing like the strong baritone he had commanded back in Minnesota.

"Our pesty friend here," the General waved vaguely in my direction, "has found out about the cloning. Now he thinks I'm responsible for the deaths of Joseph and Jerome ... and for Dr. Klienerman and that Secret Service agent."

Peña turned his head slowly from the General toward me. "That is nonsense."

"Who killed them, then?" I asked.

His chest rose and fell twice before he answered, still in a breathless whisper, "Why assume ... they were ... killed? I told you ..."

"You told me the two duplicates of the President died of unknown causes."

"Yes . . ."

"Does that sound like a natural death? Do people normally just—turn off, stop living? Isn't there always some *cause* of death? Heart attack? Stroke? Cancer? Gunshot wound? Something?"

"Usually . . . but . . ."

The General broke in. "You don't understand the situation at all, dammit! Stop browbeating the man."

"Then *you* explain it. You tell me what the situation is."

He glowered at me. "I still want to know just what in the hell is pushing you, Albano. What's in this for you? What do you want?"

For an instant I got a mental picture of retiring in luxury to some South Pacific atoll. And the next instant I saw myself in the lagoon with cement boots and a delegation of sharks coming to destroy the evidence.

"This may sound kind of hokey to you," I said, "but I shook hands with the President of the United States and agreed to do the best I could to help him be the best damned President he could be. Somebody's trying to kill him, or replace him, or fuck up his name so thoroughly that he'll have to step down. I want to prevent that from happening. That's what's pushing me."

"And you think I want to kill my own son? Or hurt him in any way?"

"You tell me."

Dr. Peña fumbled under his caftan and pulled out a face mask. He clamped it over his nose and mouth. Oxygen. He waved feebly with his free hand, telling us to continue.

"You were saying that I don't understand the situation," I said to the General. "So explain it to me."

He gave Peña a worried glance, then hunched forward in his chair and stared hard at me. "You know how I acquired control of North Lake Labs, I suppose."

"We figured it out."

"Nothing really illegal about it, you realize, although

I suppose some purists might rant about conflict of interest."

"You weren't the first Pentagon officer who made himself rich." Oh, goodness, was I being tough.

He grunted. "Do you know *why* I bought North Lake?"

"To get rich quick."

A sardonic smile this time. "Sure. And do you know why I wanted to get rich?"

I shrugged.

"To help make my son President."

"Oh. That."

"Yes," he said. "That. Every man wants his son to be President, right? It's the great American fantasy. But I knew how to make it happen. I *knew!* I needed three things: money, and lots of it; a laboratory facility that I could control absolutely; and this wonderful old man here, Alfonso Peña."

"So you made a son and had him cloned."

"Exactly. And do you know why? Do you understand why he *had* to be cloned? Why there had to be more than one James J. Halliday?"

I started to think about that one, but the General didn't wait for my retarded thought processes.

"I didn't just want my son to go into politics," he said, edging forward eagerly in his leather chair. "I wanted him to be President! Which meant he had to be a better politician than anyone else. And more knowledgeable about economics. About defense. About foreign policy, and labor, and commerce, and welfare, and everything else that the President gets hit with."

It was starting to dawn on me.

He bounced up from the chair and started pacing the room, face glowing with ancient excitement, arms gesticulating.

"Look at the Presidents we've had before him! Half of them were clowns who didn't know anything—not a damned thing—except how to win an election campaign. Public relations candidates! Once they were in office they turned into marionettes, run by whoever got closest to them, manipulated by their own White House staffs.

"And the other half ... even worse. Single-minded ideologues and fanatics. Jurgenson and his New Capitalism. Fourteen million permanently unemployed and he's building a retirement villa for himself on public funds. No wonder there were food riots. And that idiot Neo-Socialist Marcusi ... I still think he was a Mafia candidate ..."

"So you were going to produce the perfect President," I said.

"Damned right!" He pounded a fist into his palm. "A candidate who knew more about the problems *and* *solutions* than any single human being could possibly know. A candidate who had all the time he needed to make the right political contacts, and all the time he needed to learn everything there was to know about every problem area of the Presidency. The perfect candidate and the perfect President."

"Each member of the clone group is an expert in a different field," I said.

The General nodded hard enough to send a lock of iron-gray hair down over his forehead. His eyes were bright. "The boys were trained from childhood, from the time they were old enough to read. They knew their mission."

"How many of them were there?" I asked.

"Eight. Eight brothers ... James John Halliday and his seven identical brothers. My son. My sons. Eight sons—and one. Eight bodies and brains, but all the same. My only son—the President of the United States."

"They were not ... totally identical," Dr. Peña's weak voice whispered.

The General frowned. "Yes, sure. Not fully identical, no more than identical twins are exactly the same. They all looked and acted alike, but each one of them is a little different from the others. They all have their own little quirks. The psychologists claim ..."

"One of them," Peña gasped, "died . . . in childhood."

"Died? Of what?"

"Doesn't matter," the General said, annoyed. "He died of natural causes."

But Dr. Peña, his oxygen mask fallen to his lap, said, "Smallpox. He died . . . of smallpox."

"*What?*"

"The inoculation . . . when we vaccinated him . . . his body failed to develop the immunological response . . . instead of developing . . . an immunity to the disease . . . he died from it."

The General seemed angry again. "But the others were all healthy, perfectly sound. There's always a runt in every litter."

Peña seemed to want to say something more, but instead he fumbled for his oxygen mask and lifted it up to his face.

"So there were seven brothers—identical septuplets—running the campaign for the Presidency."

"That's right," the General said. "You've dealt mainly with James John, the first of them. He's the public-image maker. He makes the political speeches, handles the personal contacts. He's good at it."

"Damned good," I said.

"On occasions, as I understand it, you've dealt with James Jackson and James Jason—economics and foreign policy. And Jerome—science policy. He's the one who died in Boston. Johnny had to give Jerome's science speech for him. If those two cops hadn't surprised my men in the alley there . . ." His voice trailed off. Might have beens.

"And I thought it was just moodiness, or the pressures of the day," I said, more to myself than to him. "I never knew the difference from one to the other."

"Nobody does. Nobody except Robert Wyatt and a dozen of *my* people who work inside the White House."

"Which is why security has always been so tight around him."

"Not security. Privacy." The General's mouth curled slightly. "It wouldn't do to have somebody like you burst into the Oval Office and see three or four Presidents conferring with each other."

"Jesus Christ," I muttered.

"So there you are," said the General. "No plot. No cabal. No attempt to kill the President and slide in a phony look-alike."

"But two of the clones have died."

"Three," said Dr. Peña.

I turned to him. "Three? Besides the one who died in infancy?"

"Yesterday . . . in Washington. When I got the news . . . I must have collapsed."

The General's face clouded again. "It was Jason. They've shipped the body to North Lake."

"How . . . how did it happen?" I asked.

"Same as the others," the General said. "He was working in his office in the subbasement of the White House and they found him collapsed at his desk. The body was still warm."

Suddenly I was on my feet. "Somebody's methodically killing each one of them."

But the General grabbed my wrist and yanked me back down to my chair. "Stop looking for plots under every piece of furniture, dammit!"

"But . . ."

"Look at me," he commanded. "Do you think for one instant that if I thought somebody was killing my sons, *my son,* I'd sit here and let the bastards get away with it? Or the President would allow his own brothers to be murdered without finding out who was doing it and nailing him? Do you think this planet's big enough for such a murderer to hide in? It's not."

Finally I was beginning to understand why the President had kept the investigation so small, so tightly secret. It was a family affair, and no outsiders were wanted or needed.

"But what's killing them?"

"They're dying of the same thing that killed Jesse, in

infancy. Somehow . . ." and he looked at Dr. Peña as he spoke, "somehow their immunological systems are breaking down. Their bodies can't protect them from germs or viruses. Their biochemistry is screwed up and they die from the slightest infection . . . anything, a scratch, a common cold could kill them. Somebody sneezing in the same room."

A clatter made me turn back to the doctor. He had let the oxygen mask fall to the floor.

"No," he said, as strongly as he could. It was only a harsh whisper. "That is not true! They are not . . . it cannot be true."

"Alfonso, nobody's blaming you . . ."

Dr. Peña shook his head from side to side. "No, my old friend. You do not understand. We have checked. We have performed tests. The immune defenses of the body . . . do not suddenly disappear . . . They cannot."

The General went to his side. "Now don't excite yourself."

"But . . . you must listen!" Peña could barely get enough breath into him to wheeze out the words. He lifted one frail hand and pointed at me. "He . . . he is more correct . . . than you are. They . . . they are not just dying . . . they are being killed . . . murdered . . ."

"But how?" the General demanded. "You said yourself that there was no sign of violence. No poison. The deaths were from infections . . . they were natural. *Natural!*"

"No." The doctor's voice seemed to be coming from far away. "They . . . are being . . . murdered."

His head lolled back. His mouth sagged open. His chest stopped heaving. General Halliday looked up at me, and damned if there weren't tears in his eyes.

CHAPTER FOURTEEN

Only twice in my life have people close to me died. Both times by chance I was out of town when it happened. And I stayed away. I avoided the wakes, the funerals, the sobbing relatives and somber friends. It all seemed so pointless, so futile. Maybe I was scared, deep inside. Maybe I saw myself in the coffin, or was afraid I would.

I stayed for Peña's funeral. I'm not sure why, but I stayed. The General's people did it all very swiftly and efficiently. The old man was buried in the woods behind the General's main house. They had to clear off the thinning layer of snow that was still on the ground to dig the grave. The soil was frozen; the digging was hard work.

It was a very small band of mourners. The General, Robert Wyatt, a few of the General's hired hands, Peter Thornton from North Lake—trying not to look pleased that he was now in charge of the lab—and me.

And the President.

A local minister said a few hushed words and they lowered Peña's coffin into the ground. I knew instinctively that there were already three other graves under the snow, with flat little markers that said "J. J. Halliday." A fourth one would be dug soon.

That night the General, Wyatt, the President, and I ate a quiet dinner together. Thornton had flown back to Minnesota immediately after the burial service. The

President turned out to be James Jeffrey, the specialist in defense policy.

I still couldn't quite get it through my skull that he was one of eight identical clone brothers; one of four remaining brothers. Hell, he was the President! Every bone, every fold of skin, every gesture, every nuance of voice: the President. His eyes, the way his hair flopped over his forehead, the kind of grin he gave me as he kidded me about reading the old Watergate tapes for a lesson in how *not* to cover up a White House secret. He was the President, the only one I'd known. There couldn't be another one just like him. My brain and guts and soul refused to accept the idea. He couldn't be one of a set of eight. Or seven. Or four.

We were pretty somber as we sat down to eat in the oak-paneled dining room. But as that same robotlike Oriental butler served us steaks, Jeffrey began telling his father about the arguments he had been having with his brothers over the Iran-Kuwait war.

"We've got to be ready to go in there," he said fervently, "in force. We've got to be able to protect our own interests."

The General nodded agreement. I worked on my steak and kept quiet.

"But do you think Johnny understands that?" Jeffrey grumbled. "He's more worried about losing a few votes in Congress than losing the whole Middle East."

"John knows the political infighting," the General said. "If he doesn't think . . ."

"I've made my own assessment of the politics," Jeffrey interrupted. "I've dealt with the Senate committees. And the House, too. I could swing the Hill, if John would give me a chance to try."

The General looked up from his plate. "It's John's job to make the political decisions. If he thinks the Congress would block you, you'd better go along with his estimate of the situation."

Jeffrey cocked his head slightly to one side. Just like the President. *Dummy!* I hollered at myself. *He* is *the President. One-eighth of the Presidency, at least.*

With that smile I knew so well, the smile that meant he was going to say something unpleasant but didn't want you to get upset about it, Jeffrey answered his father. "I don't think John's qualified to make this decision. He doesn't understand the details of the military situation as well as I do. Nor the economic situation, for that matter."

They discussed—or argued, depending on your boil-over threshold—the situation right through dessert. Just a quiet little family debate. Like father and son arguing over who's going to use the family car tonight. Except that the son was the President of the United States, the subject was whether or not we will enter the Iran-Kuwait war, and the men he was arguing against were his identical clone brothers who were back in Washington.

My brain was telling me that I had to accept the reality of the situation. But the rest of me still didn't want to deal with it. You can know something is true, intellectually, and accept it and even deal with the reality as part of your world-view, on which you base your work. But that doesn't mean you *believe* it's true, down at the deepest level of your existence. Inside me, in that special subbasement where I keep all my old Sunday school lessons and nightmare terrors and fantasy desires, down there the real, secret, deepest *me* hadn't yet accepted what my brain had already filed away in one of its neat little storage cabinets. I knew the President had been cloned, and there were four identical brothers in the White House. I knew there had been seven, up to a few months ago. I knew it.

But I didn't believe it.

I flew back to Washington that night in one of the General's private supersonic jets with the President. We sat side by side in the most luxurious reclining chairs I'd ever flown in, and watched the television screen built into the forward bulkhead of the passenger compartment. The President was delivering a speech, live, from the White House. He was signing the new Economic Incentives Act, and taking the opportunity to coax the Congress for even more action on his domestic programs.

At forty-two thousand feet above the prairie wheat basket of the nation, I sat beside the President and watched the President on TV, live.

"... and although this act will go a long way toward turning urban adults into taxpaying, productive citizens rather than welfare recipients, we still have a long way to go on education and day care facilities for the young people of the core cities ..." Carrot and stick. That patented Halliday smile and the constant urging to do more, go further, dare higher.

"They say the poor are always with us," the President concluded. "Perhaps that's because those who are not poor have never put their whole hearts and minds to the task of eradicating poverty. We have the wealth, we have the technology, we have the knowledge to lift the blight of poverty from our cities and countryside. The question is, do we have the heart, the soul, the will to do it? That is a question that not even the President can answer, my fellow citizens. Only you can answer it. Thank you. Good night and God bless you."

I turned my head as the image faded on the screen and saw the President grinning to (at?) himself. "He's got style, John has," Jeffrey told me. "I've got to deliver a speech on defense policy next week at West Point. I'll never be able to put it across the way he does." He sounded almost wistful.

"Look at it this way," I suggested. "Nobody's noticed the difference between you."

That made him happy. I tried to get him to talk about the deaths of his brothers, whether he felt they were natural or not. He evaded my attempts, finally cranking his chair back and closing his eyes in a convenient nap.

When we landed, I saw how ridiculously easy it is for a man who looks exactly like the President to get through National Airport and into the White House without being detected. The plane merely taxied to a small private hangar, and we stepped from the jet's hatch to a waiting limousine. The only people in the hangar were the plane's two-man crew, the chauffeur, and two armed security guards. All of them were General Halliday's hand-picked employees.

Jeffrey dropped me off at my apartment building before going on to the White House. The limousine had one-way windows, so no one could see into it, and he stayed back in the shadows when I opened the door and quickly hopped out. Barring an automobile accident, there was no way for anyone to see him. The chauffeur drove slowly, and he had Secret Service credentials; the limousine was built like a tank, and its license plate bore the special White House code. They'd have to run over Abraham Lincoln before anyone could pry The Man out of the back seat. And there were unmarked cars gliding along in front and behind us as well. No noise, no sirens. But the limousine was well escorted.

When I finally stumbled into my apartment, I felt suddenly drained, emotionally and physically washed out. I let my flight-weight travel kit clunk to the floor of the living room, made my way to the bathroom for a fast leak, and was already halfway out of my suit when I turned on the bedroom light.

Vickie was in my bed, rubbing her eyes like a kid who's been awakened by her loutish parents' party.

"You're back . . ." she mumbled sleepily.

"What the hell are you doing here?" I'm nothing if not gracious when surprised.

She pulled herself up to a sitting position. She was wearing a nightgown, but it was flimsy, transparent.

"I thought this would be a safe place. With you out of town, nobody'd think to look for me here."

I sat on the bed beside her.

"Besides," she said, "I wanted to be here when you got back."

She leaned slightly toward me, and I kissed her. I didn't feel tired anymore.

"I was worried about you," she said.

"I called the office every day."

"But you didn't talk with me."

"I thought it'd be better if I didn't."

All this while I was holding her, kissing her, and squirming out of my clothes at the same time. If I didn't wrench my back then, I never will.

Between making love and making talk, bringing her up to date on what had happened at Aspen, it was damned near dawn before we fell asleep. And Vickie hadn't shut off my radio alarm. It started floating Beethoven at us at 7:30 sharp.

We showered together, I shaved while she dried her hair, I dressed while she put on makeup, and I flailed the last four eggs in the refrigerator into breakfast while she dressed. For kicks I sliced the butt end of an old pepperoni and tossed it in with the eggs. Start the day with a bang.

After breakfast we grabbed our respective handbags and went to the elevator. Vickie reached for the Lobby button, but I pushed her hand away and punched R, for roof. She started to ask me why, but I put a finger to my lips.

When we got to the roof and stepped out into the fine spring morning, I walked her to the parapet at the edge, as far from the door, and any listening devices, as we could get.

"I want to bring Hank Solomon up to date on what's happening, but I'll be damned if I know how to get in touch with him without tipping off whoever's watching us. They most likely know he's in with us, but still . . ."

Vickie shaded her eyes from the sun. "Do you think we're still being bugged?"

I nodded. "This thing isn't over yet. Far from it. Peña's death may have been natural, but none of the others was. Maybe it wasn't the General who did it, but it's somebody close to him."

"Wyatt?"

"Could be."

"Why?"

"If I knew that, I'd know for sure if it was him or not."

"So what do we do?"

"That's what I want to ask Hank about. He ought to know more about this kind of thing than we do."

"He told me he'd find a way to contact you. You shouldn't try to reach him."

"You saw him? When?"

Vickie grinned. "Very tricky stuff. I got a letter at the office, addressed to me personally. All that was inside was a clipping from a newspaper, with ads for the movies on it. One theater's selection was circled in red, and the time of the showing was underlined. The envelope was from the Treasury Department, so I assumed it was from Hank ... Secret Service is in Treasury."

"So he met you at the theater."

"That's right. For about three minutes. He told me he was keeping a watch on me. And that he'd get in touch with you when you got back."

I found myself taking a deep breath and half wishing I had stayed in Boston. Not even Beacon Hill politics was as devious as all this.

We drove to the office together, and by the time the elevator had stopped at our floor, Vickie had put on her office personality. Just a sunny smile and a "Have a good day!" Not that I made a grab for her. I had my office personality on, too. It had been warm and good in bed; it was great to have her there when I got home, rather than an empty apartment. *But don't start to expect it,* I warned myself. *Or depend on it.*

I got a lot of kidding from the press corps at the morning briefing about being a gentleman of leisure. But no undercurrent of worry or rumor that my recent absences might be a symptom of something cooking inside the White House. If a Cabinet officer or a Pentagon official started playing hookey, then there'd be rumbles of interest from the newshawks. But the press secretary? Nobody cared.

As the briefing broke up, His Holiness told me that

The Man wanted me in the Oval Office at 5:30. I made a mental note and went back to the Aztec Temple to plow through the accumulated paperwork on my desk.

Hank Solomon was one of the security guards down at the inspection post under the West Wing that afternoon. He winked at me, and I did my best not to make it look as if I knew him as I stepped through the sensor arch that screened me for identification and weapons.

The President was behind his big, curved desk as I stepped into the Oval Office. Wyatt was sitting in my favorite chair, the Scandinavian slingback, so I took his usual standby, the rocker next to the fireplace.

The Man watched me as I sat down. He grinned. "I can see exactly what's going through your mind," he said.

"Sir?"

"You're wondering, *Which one is he?* Right?"

I grinned back at him. "Yes . . . that's right."

"I'm James John, the one whose hand you shook when you agreed to take the job."

Somehow I felt relieved.

"It's no use staring at him," Wyatt groused. "You won't be able to tell the difference between them. *I* can't, for God's sake, and I've known them since childhood."

"What're we going to do about this?" I blurted.

The President's smile faded. "The deaths, you mean."

"The *murders*," I said. "Somebody's killing you—your brothers, one by one."

Wyatt stirred uncomfortably. "That's not . . ."

"Don't give me that 'natural causes' crap again!" My voice was rising. So was my blood pressure. "Maybe the General believes that, but I don't. Peña didn't either. I was there when he tried to convince the General."

"Peña was an old, *old* man," Wyatt said. "I think

maybe he went senile, right there at the end. Too many shocks. After all . . ."

"He would know better than anyone else," I insisted.

The President shook his head. "Meric . . . murder has got to have a motivation. If somebody's killing us, who is it? And why?"

I swear the words were out of my mouth before I realized that my mind had come to that conclusion. "It's one of your brothers," I said. "The one who wants to be the *only* President of the United States."

For what seemed like fifteen minutes there was absolute silence in the Oval Office. Wyatt sat like a marble statue, completely unmoving and emotionless. The President looked thoughtful; then his face clouded darkly. And my own brain was telling me, *Yes! That's the answer! It's the only possible answer. One of them is killing the others. One of them wants this office, this power, this nation all for himself. One of them is insane.*

Wyatt finally stirred himself. "If you think . . ."

But the President silenced him with the slightest lift of one finger. "Robert, it's the same conclusion I came to weeks ago."

The old man looked truly shocked. "What?"

"I think it's time we brought this all out into the open," the President said. "Time to clear the air."

He pushed his chair back from the desk and got to his feet. We automatically got up, too.

"Come with us, Meric," said The Man.

Wyatt seemed to understand what he was going to do. "Wait up a minute . . . he's not family."

The President smiled sardonically. "He is now. He knows as much about us as anyone. Come on, Meric."

We went out the side door of the office, down to the basement, past the inspection station where Hank still stood on duty, and along the West Wing to the private elevator. Wyatt pushed the button, the doors slid open as if the machine had been waiting all day to be called on, and we followed the President into the tiny, red-wood-paneled elevator cab.

There were no tourists in the White House at this hour of the afternoon, of course, but we rode in the windowless elevator past the ground and first floors and got off in the quiet main corridor of the second floor, the sacrosanct living quarters for the President and his First Lady.

Wordlessly, The Man paced along the richly carpeted hallway and led us to the Lincoln Sitting Room. I had never seen it before, although I knew which room it was, right next to the Lincoln Bedroom. I had seen both of them in photographs.

But when the President opened the door, it wasn't the *fin de siècle* furniture or the ornate draperies that hit me. Three more James J. Hallidays were already in the room: one by the window, sitting in a green velvet-covered chair; another at the scroll desk, tapping out something on a computer terminal's keyboard; the third standing by the portrait of Chester Arthur that hung on the far wall.

I gulped.

The President—the one I had come upstairs with—grabbed me by the elbow and pulled me toward the middle of the room. Pointing, he introduced: "That's Jeffrey, scowling alongside President Arthur. And Jackson, jiggling the national debt figures. And Joshua, by the window. You've met all three of them before."

They nodded or smiled at me. But Joshua said nervously, "Why bring an outsider into this? There's been enough trouble already, hasn't there?"

"Meric's not an outsider," John said. "And if we want to keep our troubles out of the public view, we're going to need Meric's continued wholehearted cooperation."

Joshua didn't reply, but it was clear that he wasn't happy to see me up there in their private clubroom.

"What's going on, John?" Jeffrey asked. "Why the melodramatics?"

I was still goggle-eyed. All of them looked exactly alike. Their voices were the same. The trim of their hair. The way they gestured with their hands. The only discernible difference was their clothing. Jeffrey, the defense expert, was wearing a simple one-piece tan jumpsuit. Jackson, the economist, wore a more conservative dark blue shirtjac and slacks, while Joshua—whose main interest was natural resources and agricultural policy—had a yellow sportshirt over pseudosuede jeans. A soldier, a banker, and a farmer. I tried to fix them in my mind that way. James John—*the* President, I kept thinking—wore his usual work clothes: dark slacks, comfortable boots, and an open-neck light shirt.

Wyatt took a chair near the door and I drifted, weak-kneed, toward the windows as James John answered.

"We've all been trying to hide from the facts. I think it's time we faced up to them. The deaths haven't been natural. They were murders."

Jackson looked up from his computer keyboard. "No way, John. If Peña couldn't find any signs . . ."

"Peña was convinced it was murder," John said. "He couldn't figure out how it was done, but he knew it was murder."

"No, I don't believe that," Jackson said. "Peña was just emotionally unable to accept the fact that his work . . . well . . . it's failing."

Jeffrey said tightly, "Each of us might go just as the others did."

"No," John said. "I don't believe that." It was like hearing an echo of Jackson's words from a moment earlier.

"Sure, you can afford to disbelieve it," said Joshua. "You're the natural, the firstborn. Whatever it is probably won't affect you."

"That's not so," John answered. The voice was still calm, but there was an edge to it.

Wyatt said, "You're all genetically identical. What happens to one of you, as far as your body chemistry is concerned, will happen to you all. Lord, you all got the mumps at the same time when you were kids, and it lasted exactly the same number of days for each of you. Like clockwork. John's not immune to anything that the rest of you are susceptible to."

"That's only theory, Robert," Jeffrey said. "Everything about cloning processes is totally new ... nobody's done it before with human beings. We're the first."

I was starting to see differences among them. Slight differences in nuance, in character. They were four identical brothers all right. But just like identical twins, although they looked alike on the outside, they saw the world differently, and the insides of their heads were far from identical.

Wyatt was saying, "We could keep you in a germ-free environment, back at the lab. Then you wouldn't have to worry ..."

"That's impossible!" Jackson snapped. "How in hell can we function in the Presidency from a germ-free cell at North Lake? It's tough enough playing this seven-man shuffle—"

"Four-man shuffle," Jeffrey corrected. "We're down to four now."

John was still standing in the middle of the room. He raised his hands for silence.

"Now, listen," he said. "I've been giving the matter a lot of thought. The deaths were not natural. They were murders."

Jackson shook his head but kept silent. Joshua seemed to tense forward in his chair. Jeffrey, who was nearest me, asked quietly: "So what are we going to do about it, John?"

"Find out which one of us is the murderer."

I think my heart actually stopped beating. For what seemed like an eternity, nothing stirred in the room. Not even the dust motes in the slanting sunlight from the windows seemed to move. Everything froze.

Finally Jeffrey found his voice. "What ... did you say?"

I'd never seen such an expression on the President's face before. It must have been the way Lincoln looked when he learned of the carnage at Gettysburg.

"It's one of us," John said, his voice deceptively level. "No one else could be doing it. One of us is systematically killing the others. One of us wants to be the sole occupant of that office down in the West Wing."

They looked back and forth among themselves. No one spoke. Wyatt seemed to be in a state of shock, ashen-faced, immobile, staring at the floor. I could see the wheels working inside those four identical heads. They recognized the truth of it. Maybe each of them had suspected it from the first, but pushed it away. Now it was out in the open. They could no longer ignore it.

"One of us wants to be the only President of the United States," John repeated.

"I can't . . ." Joshua started, then lapsed back into silence.

"It does make some sense," Jackson admitted.

Jeffrey said, "But . . . killing his own brothers. It's horrible . . . he'd have to be insane."

John nodded. "I suppose so. But power can corrupt, we all know that. There've been enough murderous families in history to drive the point home. And we've done a few kinky acts here and there . . . we're not immune to the disease."

"It can't be!" Joshua said firmly. "I just won't believe it. Not unless you can show me how the murders were done. Hell, we don't even know that they *were* murders."

"Wrong, Josh," said John softly. "I know."

Wyatt looked up at him. "Tell me. Tell me how it was done and make it convincing, because I don't think I could ever believe that one of you boys is killing the others."

"It's very simple," John said. "I merely asked myself how I'd go about killing the rest of us. Once I became convinced that they were murders, I tried to work out

in my head what *I* would have done if I'd wanted to
murder my brothers. It didn't take long to figure it out.
Just the past few days . . . that's all the time I
needed."

"And?"

"The key was Jesse."

"He died nearly forty years ago."

"Yes, but how did he die?"

Wyatt answered, "From a breakdown of his body's
immunological defenses. He lost his immunities to disease germs. The only way he could have been saved
would have been to put him in a germ-free chamber,
but we didn't recognize that until it was too late."

John nodded agreement. "And Joe, Jerry, and Jason
all died the same way. All body immunities suddenly
gone. Common cold germs became fatal to them."

No one moved. No one answered. We all focused on
John so intently that an ICBM attack could have hit
Washington and we'd never have known it.

"I checked with North Lake a week ago," John said.
"Put in a scrambled call to their contracts department.
They gave me a list of the research contracts they're
now working on for the Defense Department. One of
them is for the development of a mutated virus that
breaks down the human body's immunological systems.
It's top-secret work. Access to information about it is
limited to only a handful of people in the Pentagon."
He almost smiled, sadly. "I had to remind the man I
spoke with that I'm the Commander-in-Chief."

"A virus that breaks down the body's immune systems?"

"Nontraceable," John said. "Apparently the Defense
Intelligence Agency wants to develop the virus as a
standby for 'perfect' assassinations. No visible cause of
death. The victim just stops living. Any germs in his
body can multiply out of control and kill him in less
than a day."

"Jesus Christ."

"And you've known about this for a week?" I
asked.

John gave a helpless shrug. "I've worried over it for a week. I guess I didn't want to face reality. You forced me to bring it out into the light of day, Meric."

"This virus is being developed for the Defense Department?" Joshua asked.

"I didn't know anything about it," Jeffrey snapped.

"Nobody's saying you did," John answered.

"This virus," Wyatt asked, "it's been tested? It works?"

"It's been used on primate apes and other lab animals. Totally successful. One hundred percent fatal. The North Lake people haven't tried it on human beings, for obvious reasons . . ."

"But you're saying," Wyatt's voice trembled badly, "that one of you boys—one of you in this room—got his hands on samples of this virus and used it . . . used it to . . ." His voice cracked altogether. He buried his face in his hands.

John stepped over to him and put a hand on his shoulder. "We have to face the facts, Robert. It's what I would do, if I wanted to be the only resident of this house. And we all think pretty much alike, don't we?"

"That's for sure," Jackson said.

"So—what do we do?" Joshua asked, his voice pitched higher than the others'.

Jeffrey gave a sharp, bitter laugh that was almost a cough. "It's simple. We wait until there's only one of us left, and he's the guilty one."

"Or," John countered, "we let the guilty one know that we're aware of what he's doing, and how he's doing it, and we ask him to come forward and admit it."

They looked uneasily at one another.

"I think we all know that whoever's doing it is mentally unbalanced," John said. "We won't punish him. We want to take care of him, cure him. Whichever one of us it is, he's our brother. We want to help him, not punish him."

No one moved, except to search one another's eyes for an admission of guilt.

Finally Joshua said, "We'd better bring the General out here. Maybe he can get to the bottom of this."

Wyatt shook his head. "No . . . he's an old man. He's not as tough as he pretends to be. If he ever found out about this . . ."

Jackson said, "If he ever finds out that we went through this *without* bringing him in on it, it might kill him."

Jeffrey grinned ruefully. "Or he might kill the rest of us."

John said to Wyatt, "Robert, you'd better go out to Aspen and tell him about this. In person. No phone calls. See what he wants to do."

"He'll come boiling back here at Mach Five," Wyatt said.

"All right. If that's what he wants to do, we won't stand in his way." He turned to his brothers. "Right?"

"No way we could stop him," Jackson admitted.

"Someone should check out North Lake Labs," Joshua said. "It might be possible to find out who took the virus samples."

"Ridiculous!" Jeffrey snapped. "Even if one of us was foolish enough to acquire the virus cultures in person—which I doubt—he wouldn't have given his correct name. None of the lab people can tell us apart. Not even Peña could."

"I suppose so," Joshua admitted. "We used to play all sorts of tricks on him," he said to me wistfully.

But John said, "We should check out the lab, though. I'll get Pournelle at the FBI to take charge of that end of things personally."

"You're not going to tell him about us?" Jackson asked sharply.

"Of course not," John said. "But I want to find out who made off with that virus sample."

"If anybody did."

"Somebody must have. And Pournelle's people can find out who and when. Then we find the man and talk to him ourselves."

"If it was a man," Jackson said, with a slight smirk. "You're lapsing into male chauvinism, Johnny. Don't do that in front of the voters."

They all laughed. Somehow it annoyed me.

"Hold it!" I heard myself shout at them.

They stopped and turned toward me, four identical looks of polite amusement, four faces saying, *What's the hired man doing, yelling at us?*

"It's not good enough," I said.

"What's not?"

I had to face them down. All of them. "You're still treating this as if it's a family squabble."

"Isn't it?"

"Hell, no! It's still a plot to kill the President, as far as I'm concerned."

"Meric, we're taking the strongest action we can," John said. "You don't want us to do anything that will tip off the press to our ... brotherhood, do you? That would ruin everything. I'd have to ... *we'd* have to resign the Presidency."

"That would put Lazar in the White House."

"This nation's not ready for a Jewish President."

"Not with the Middle East at war again."

I stood my ground. They were making me sore, tinkering with the Presidency, the nation, the whole goddamned world as if it were a private family affair.

"I don't care what you say," I told them. "This isn't enough. Checking North Lake Labs and sitting around here chatting with each other. For Chrissakes, one of you has killed three of your brothers!"

"That's our business," Jeffrey said, glaring at me.

"The hell it is! It's mine, and every other citizen's, too."

"What are you trying to say, Meric?"

I really didn't know, but as usual my mouth worked

faster than my brain. "It just isn't going to be enough. The steps you're taking ... they won't tell you a god-damned thing. Not until it's too late. The murderer can wipe out all three of you overnight, if he wants to, while you're still futzing around checking records at North Lake or consulting with the General."

Jackson started to say something, but John hushed him.

"What do you suggest?" John asked.

"No suggestion. Action. I'm going to call a press conference in forty-eight hours. Two days from now. And I'm going to spill my guts to whoever'll listen. Unless you've got the murderer before then."

"You can't do that!" Jackson snapped.

"Try and stop me."

"The murderer will try," John said almost sadly. "I think, Meric, for your own safety's sake, you'd better reconsider."

I could see differences in their faces now. Joshua looked scared. Jackson was blazingly angry. Jeffrey was angry, too, but the smoldering kind that builds slowly and waits its chance for revenge. John looked sad, and something more—relieved? Glad that the end was in sight?

I shook my head. "No. There's no other way. Either you flush him out or I break the story. Otherwise he'll have the rest of you dead and sit down in that Oval Office all by himself. And *that's* what I'm really afraid of."

"He'll have to kill me, too," Wyatt said.

"What makes you think he wouldn't?" Jackson answered. The old man sagged back in his chair. But I had a different thought. I could see Wyatt serving the last remaining James J. Halliday, right there in the Oval Office, burying the fact that the President was a multimurderer under a ton of justifications about family duty and the nation's needs.

John took a couple of steps toward me. Quietly, he said, "Meric, if we can't talk you out of this, the least I can do is give you a Secret Service security guard. If you're going to set yourself up as a target, we might as well *try* to protect you."

"All right," I said. "How about Hank Solomon? He and I get along pretty well."

He looked at me quizzically. If I'd been really sharp, instead of just dazzled by all the high drama going on, I would have realized that mentioning Hank's name removed any doubt from the murderer's mind about who the third member of my pitiful little gang was.

But right at that moment I wasn't thinking about that at all. As I mentioned Hank's name, somehow it popped into my mind that there was one person involved in this affair that not even one of Halliday's brothers had mentioned. Neither Wyatt nor the General had ever brought up her name.

Laura. The First Lady. What did she know about all this? And whose wife was she?

CHAPTER FIFTEEN

I deliberately avoided calling Vickie when I got out of the White House. My mind was in turmoil. Too much had happened too quickly. If I was going to be a murderer's target, okay, there wasn't much I could do about it. But no need to set her up as the next clay pigeon.

Besides, it would be too easy to get damned romantic about the danger of it all, and start acting like some asinine shiny-armored knight and make a real idiot of myself. Vickie was an adult; she didn't need me in her life. I'd bring her nothing but grief.

Okay, she was good to be with; she brightened up a room and brought warmth to my life. She was fine in bed. *And keep thinking with your gonads instead of your brains,* I warned myself, *and you'll both end up on the next cold-storage shipment to Minnesota.*

As I thought about it, in the cab on my way back to my apartment, I doubted that the murderer would use the same technique on me that he had on his brothers. But he didn't have to, of course. Hell, he was the President! He could get rid of me in a thousand ways, from a fatal accident to a nuclear strike. Even if I wanted to bow out gracefully and exile myself in Afghanistan, he'd never believe it. He'd send someone looking for me—a clean-cut, reliable, terribly loyal assassin.

So it was a nasty shock when I opened the door to my apartment and found Hank Solomon sitting there, reading a magazine.

"Jesus Suffering Christ!" I swung the door shut behind me. As I calmed down from the shock of fear at seeing a potential assassin waiting for me, I griped, "Does everybody in creation have the combination to my front door?"

"Only us friendly helpers and bodyguards," Hank said easily.

"You got here pretty damned fast," I said, not yet ready to forgive him for scaring me.

"When the President his own self calls yew, yew move your butt, buddy. Yew got friends in high places."

"And enemies."

"Yep. Guess that's so. What's been happenin'?"

I hesitated and he told me the room was clear of bugs. How he knew was beyond me; he couldn't have had more than a few minutes alone in the room before I came in. But my faith in modern electronics was strong enough to take him at his word. So I told him what had happened in the Lincoln Sitting Room.

Hank listened without emitting so much as a grunt until I was finished. Then he said, "Well, ol' buddy, yew kinda put me right there on the spot alongside yew, dintcha?"

I admitted that I had. He grinned and said, "Okay, least yew can do is take me out t' dinner. And we can stop in a post office along th' way."

"Post office?"

He had already unfolded himself out of the seat and gone to the door. "Yep. Make a tape recording of everything yew just tole me and mail it to a few trustable friends with orders not t' open it 'til Christmas ... or your untimely demise, whichever comes first."

"You've got a helluva way of cheering up a guy."

But the idea made sense. I thought about Len Ryan, then decided that Johnny Harrison, back in Boston, would be less tempted to ignore my instructions and listen to the tape prematurely. And I knew a couple of good men overseas in London and Kyoto.

*   *   *

It wasn't difficult to get to see Laura. The next morning, as soon as I got into the office, I went over the assignments involving her. She was addressing a special meeting of delegates from Working Office Women who were joining in the big Neo-Luddite rally at the Capitol Building to protest the loss of jobs to automation.

I called the kid who was assigned to handle the meeting's press relations and told her that I was coming along. She got the impression that I had my eye on her, and there was a promotion in the air. I didn't disillusion her.

The next thing I did was call Vickie in to set up my press conference for the following afternoon.

"You?" she asked, surprised. "A personal press conference?"

"That's right. Make certain that all the wire services and the international reps get the word."

"We'll have to tell them the subject."

"No," I shook my head. "Just tell them it's the most important story of their lives, and it's too hot to even name the subject beforehand."

She leaned back in her chair. "You're going to tell them about the President."

"Either that or get thrown out of town for canceling the conference at the last minute."

"Or get killed," Vickie said, very matter-of-factly. No histrionics.

"If that happens," I said, trying to stay equally controlled, "the story will break right away. Last night I sent tapes of the whole thing to a few trusted newsmen, with instructions to do nothing unless I die or disappear."

"And tomorrow's press conference . . ."

"Either they nail the murderer by tomorrow afternoon, or I blow the whistle."

"They'll kill you," Vickie said. "They'll kill all of us."

"No," I said again. "They won't touch you because I haven't told you what I know. I'm keeping you in the clear. You'll be safe."

"You're keeping me in the dark," she said, her voice rising slightly.

"For your own protection."

She slammed her hands down on the arms of the chair. "So you're going to take the whole burden on yourself. You're going to let them kill you, in the hopes that a few news people you once worked with will have the guts to publish the story and expose the President."

"They will," I said. "It wouldn't be the first time that only a couple of newsmen have stood between the people and a national catastrophe."

"Wonderful!" she said. "And in the meantime you're dead in some back alley in Georgetown."

"What do you want me to do?" I shouted back at her.

"Nothing." She got to her feet. "It's too late. You've done it all. They'll give you a big funeral, I bet."

"You just set up the press conference," I told her. "Let me do the worrying."

"Sure. Thanks for the advice. It was swell knowing you. You're a credit to your profession." And she stamped out of the room, furious.

But safe. Whoever was bugging my office now knew that Vickie was small potatoes, and didn't know enough to be dangerous. I hoped.

So she was sore at me. Probably a good thing. We'd been getting too close. Not good for either of us. And I was going to see Laura in another couple of hours.

WOW had set up its meeting at the Van Trayer. Laura spoke to the delegates in the main ballroom. The ornate crystal and chrome room was only half filled with WOW delegates—secretaries, file clerks, office managers who were inexorably being replaced by electronic memory systems, voice-operated typewriters, picture-phones, and computers.

I stood in the back of the room, alone. The news people, mostly women, were off to one side of the podium up at the front of the ballroom, taping sound and pictures. I frankly didn't recognize which of the girls up there was the one who worked for me. They all looked pretty much alike.

But Laura was something else. She wore her hair tightly pulled back, in a no-nonsense way, straight and efficient, as if she had only a couple of minutes to take care of it each day. Her suit was also an efficiency-image, neat and simple, bright enough to be attractive but absolutely without frills.

I came in toward the end of her speech. She was saying: "I'm a working woman, too, and have been all my adult life. As you all probably know, I was a dancer before I was married . . . and not such a very good one that I could afford the pampering of a star. I was just one of the 'girls'—" She put a special emphasis on the word, and a few sympathetic hisses rose from the audience. "—who had to pay her rent and buy her groceries with a pretty tiny paycheck."

She paused and smiled at them, a smile that said, *But I made it, and so can you!* "And if you think that being the First Lady isn't a full-time job, then guess again. I'm still a working woman, and proud of it."

They applauded enthusiastically.

"And I can assure you," she said, as the applause died down, "that you have a friend in the White House. More than one, in fact, because the President is vitally interested in the effect of automation on your jobs." Then she added, in a different tone, so that it seemed like an ad lib, "And if he weren't, he'd hear about it from me!"

More applause. Cheers. Laughter. She had them in her proverbial palm.

"As you know, the President has proposed legislation that will ease the economic burdens of job dislocations caused by automation. His motto is, 'Don't try to stop automation; try to use it.' I think that each of us here, if we really worked at it and took advantage of the new programs that the President has proposed, could become managers of one-person offices. We should be *using* these new machines to make our careers better, not resisting automation and clinging to our old dull jobs. It's time we stopped thinking of ourselves as some man's employee and started seeing ourselves as the managers and decision-makers of four-fifths of the nation's businesses. Thank you."

They rose and cheered. Maybe when they sifted through all that rhetoric and realized that only one woman out of five could possibly attain the managerial positions that Laura dangled before them, they would stop cheering. But for the moment they were solidly with her, and the President.

I made my way through the exiting crowd, getting some dirty stares from a few of the WOW delegates, and stood on the fringes of the impromptu press conference that had gathered around the First Lady. The news people ignored me; probably thought I was one of her Secret Service guards. These were mostly "Female Features" type of newspersons, not the usual White House corps, and my face meant nothing to them. The only one who seemed to recognize me was the kid from my office, whom I finally spotted after she smiled and nodded to me.

Laura fielded the newspersons' questions expertly and stood through three "special" network interviews of five minutes each, in which each of the network interviewers asked exactly the same questions. But each of the chicks could go back to her station claiming an "exclusive" interview with the First Lady. That word "exclusive" had changed its meaning a lot in the television industry.

I spotted Hank Solomon among the fringe of security men and grinned at him. He gave no indication of even noticing me. Professional ethics. I guess, in front of his peers. They were all stony-faced types and trying to melt into the background.

Finally the news people snapped shut their cameras and tape recorders and filed out of the room. I made a few nice words to the girl from my office, told her she handled things very well. She went off beaming.

When I looked around, Laura was watching me, a curious smile on her face.

"I didn't expect to see you here," she said. "When you came in, I nearly lost my place in the speech."

"I want to talk with you. In private."

She was sitting on the edge of the ballroom's dais, long legs held out straight in front of her. She gestured with a bob of her head to one of the women among her security guard. The woman looked more like a college undergrad than a Secret Service agent. Where she could have been carrying a gun under the summery little dress she had on was an intriguing mystery to me.

"Jennie," Laura asked, "can you move the team to the outside of the doors? Mr. Albano and I want to speak privately."

She nodded, just as tight-lipped and hard-eyed as the men. Inside of thirty seconds, the room was empty, but we both knew that nobody could get in with anything less than an armored squad of commandos.

Laura still had a look of casual amusement about her. "What was it you wanted to talk about, Meric?"

She had moved from the dais to one of the folding chairs in the first row of the audience. I was still on my feet, standing before her.

"I know about the cloning," I said.

"So I've heard."

"I was wondering how much you know. What ideas you have about which of them might be the murderer."

She arched an eyebrow, but said nothing.

"You agree that one of the brothers is . . . killing the rest of them?"

"I suppose that's what it is," she said. Then, looking up at me, "But it might be someone else . . . someone who wants to see just one of the brothers in power, and all the others out of the way."

"You mean Wyatt?"

She made a small shrug. "Or Lazar."

"I can't believe that."

"Or Mandella, the Secretary of Defense. Or ... anybody."

She was teasing, toying with me, not taking it seriously.

"Or you," I said suddenly.

Her smile got wider, but her eyes went cold. "Yes," she said slowly, "it might even be me. Maybe I want to be President."

"Or in total control of the President."

"It's a thought," Laura said.

It was like trying to interview a piece of sculptured crystal. Laura sat there, beautiful, smiling, *knowing*—but not giving me anything.

"I'm calling a press conference tomorrow," I said. "If there's no answer by then, I'll throw it open to the public."

"Yes. He told me."

"Who told you? Which one?"

An annoyed shake of her head. "I don't know. I make it a policy not to ask."

"You just deal with them ..."

"As if there were only one," Laura finished for me. "It's easier that way. They're careful not to let anybody see more than one at a time. They do the same for me ... most of the time."

I could feel my knees getting fluttery. "But ... but you *are* married to James John. I mean, he's the one ..."

Her eyes never faltered. She kept looking straight at me, kept her smile going, although now it was starting to look mocking. "I told you, Meric, I never ask. Was it Franklin who said, 'In the dark, all cats are gray'?"

I felt myself sit with a thump on the edge of the dais.

"Oh, don't look so shocked," Laura said, her voice getting sharp. "You'd do exactly the same thing ... men have been doing it for ages. It's called a harem."

"No ... it's not ..." I was shaking my head.

"Poor Meric. Still a Yankee frontiersman in your

head, aren't you? All the old morality. All the lovely old chauvinist attitudes."

There wasn't much I could say.

"Come here, Meric. Sit beside me." Laura patted the seat next to her.

I went over and sat, like an obedient puppy.

"You realize that if you make this story public, it will ruin the President. He'll be forced to resign."

"At least."

Laura put a finger on my lips. "Do you realize that you're doing this to hurt me? To punish me for choosing him over you?"

"You mean choosing *them,* don't you?"

"Don't be mean."

"I'm not trying to hurt you, Laura. God knows that's the last thing in the world I'd want to do."

"Then drop this press announcement. Cancel the conference."

"And let one of those brothers finish murdering the rest of them?"

"Let them settle their family matters by themselves. It doesn't concern you."

"I can't!" It sounded more like pleading than a mighty affirmation of morality, justice, and the rule of law.

"Not even for me?"

"Not even for you," I said. Miserably.

Her hand came back to my face. I could smell a fragrance that she used, a scent I hadn't known since we were in college together. She brushed at the hair over my ear.

"You don't understand what I just said, Meric," she said, very softly. "You can have me . . . if you still feel the way we used to."

"The way we used to?" My voice was a strangled squeak.

"Yes. When you loved me and I loved you. We can have that again. The two of us. Just like before."

I pulled myself away from her. "How in the hell . . . you must be out of your mind, Laura!"

Very patiently she said, "Listen to me. Jim has a little more than three years to his term. He won't try for reelection ... too much has happened for him to expect that. After he's out of office, there will be a quiet, amicable divorce. Then you and I ... together ... anywhere in the world, Meric."

There must be an instant in a heart transplant operation when the surgeons have removed your original heart but haven't yet put in the donor organ. That's how I felt right then. There was a hole in my chest, an aching cavity, livid with flame-hot pain.

"Three years ..." I heard myself mumble.

Laura said, "I never loved him, Meric. I realize that now. It was all ambition ... the power trip. And we could get together from time to time even before the three years is up. I travel a lot, and so does ..."

A sudden vision of me waiting at the end of a line, with everybody ahead of me looking like the President, snapped me back to reality.

"Sure, we could get together," I said. "With three of the brothers dead, your dance card must have a lot of holes in it."

"Don't be vicious."

"Then don't treat me like some high school kid with a hard-on. Jesus Christ, Laura, you're nothing but a high-classed whore."

"And what are you?" she snapped back, taunting. "A sniveling little boy who works at the White House and still believes everything they taught him in grammar school about patriotism and loyalty."

"Damned right I do!"

"Grow up, Meric! Be a man! It's *power* that makes the world go 'round. Power! And no matter which one of them ends up with the power in his hands alone, he'll be mine. I'll share his power."

"Yeah .. he pumps it into you, doesn't he? How the hell do you arrange it? Do they each have a certain night, or do you take them all on the same night? Do you have gang bangs in the Queen's Bedroom?"

Her smile returned, but now it was etched with acid. "Sometimes."

"Ahh, shit!" I bolted out of the chair, turned and kicked it, sending it clattering into the row of chairs behind it.

"There *are* differences among them, you know," Laura said, gloating, getting even, rising to her feet so she could pour the poison into my ears. "Even in the dark. Meric, they're each a little different."

"I don't give a damn!"

"But it's so *fascinating*. One of them likes to be sucked, one of them likes my ass. One of them—I think it's Joshua—just lets me do whatever I want to him. And then there are the parties . . . the grand balls, we call them . . ."

I should have socked her. I wanted to. Instead, I just headed up the aisle toward the exits at the back of the ballroom. Fast as I could. Nearly running.

"Meric!" she called to me.

I got to the last row of seats before I turned. I could hardly see her, my vision was blurry. I was gasping for breath. I felt like I was going to die. I wanted to.

"Cancel the press conference," Laura commanded. "We'll find the newsmen you sent those tapes to and shut them up—and you—and your two friends—one way or another."

I shook my head and staggered out of the ballroom, blubbering like a kid who's just had his last hope of joy taken away from him.

CHAPTER SIXTEEN

Hank drove me back to my apartment. My hands were shaking too badly even to hail a taxicab.

"What th' hell went on between yew two?" he asked, frank astonishment on his face. "Y'all look like somebody put yew through a meat grinder."

"Somebody did."

"Th' President's lady?"

"She's no lady."

He shrugged and weaved his way through the mounting afternoon traffic.

"Look at 'em," Hank said, more to take my mind off my troubles than anything else.

The streets were filling up with demonstrators for the big Neo-Luddite rally that was going to meet at the Capitol at sundown. The local authorities had forbidden a rally during the daylight hours, while the Capitol building was open to visitors. So the Neo-Luddite leaders found a loophole in the official decision and organized their people to congregate on the Capitol's main steps at sundown. They were expecting a hundred thousand people.

"Yew think all these people lost their jobs t' computers?" Hank asked as we threaded through cars and buses festooned with signs reading STOP AUTOMATION and PEOPLE NOT MACHINES.

"It's the second Industrial Revolution," I said. "It's happening all over again. People have been bombing computer facilities here and there."

Hank nodded. "They tell me there's even a new

kinda robot that's working foot patrol with the New York Police Department. Guess my job'll be next."

I said nothing, just watched the crowds. They seemed to be more in a holiday mood than anything else, laughing and hollering at each other. Drinking beer, inside the buses we passed.

"Maybe I oughta join 'em," Hank muttered.

"No," I said. "There's something more important for you to do. Find Vickie and get the two of you out of town. Tonight. As soon as you let me off at my place."

"Now that's a *damn* good way t' get me fired," Hank said. "My orders are t' stick with yew . . ."

"I'll be all right," I said. "They're after you and Vickie, too."

"How d'yew know?"

"What the hell do you think shook me up back there?"

His jaw dropped open. "Th' First Lady? She's in on it?"

"Deep enough to know that you two are in as deep as I am. Get Vickie and disappear. Go up to Boston and live with Johnny Harrison for the next day or two. Wait 'til after my press conference before you come back."

"But yew . . ."

"Jesus Christ Almighty! Will you do what I tell you, or do you want to get yourself killed? And Vickie too?"

"I'll get one of my buddies to fill in with yew . . ."

"No, that would tip them off. Just grab Vickie and get the hell out of town. I'll lock myself in my apartment and phone the cops if I even hear a mouse squeak."

With a shake of his head, "I dunno . . ."

"But I do. And if Vickie gets hurt I'll blame you for it."

His face tightened. "God *damn!* Life jes' gets more complicated ever' goddamned day."

"Do what I tell you," I said.

He hated the idea of leaving his assigned responsibility, but he was enough of an old-style Westerner to worry more about Vickie than about me. And I was old-fashioned enough to know that if they grabbed Vickie, I'd do whatever they told me to.

I sprinted from Hank's unmarked car to the lobby of my apartment building, waved to him through the glass doors, and went up to my rooms. The first thing I did was snoop around the place, poking into closets and even the shower stall, to make certain I was alone. The first thing after triple-locking the front door, that is. Then I put a frozen dinner in the cooker and called the door guards and told them I didn't want any visitors allowed up, under any circumstances. They could talk to me on the phone if they needed me.

I settled down with the aluminum dinner tray in my favorite living room chair and flicked on the TV. The evening news was mostly about the gathering horde of Neo-Luddites congregating at the Capitol. Congress had courageously adjourned early, so that the Congresspersons and Senators could be safely home and far from their demanding constituents. The Capitol building itself was now closed to all visitors, and there were thousands of DC and Capital police ringing the venerable old marble pile.

"Unofficial reports from generally reliable sources," the TV commentator added, "claim that the Army has several regiments of troops standing by in nearby locations, ready to deal with any emergencies that might arise."

"Generally reliable sources" was me. We had argued in the office a good part of the day about tipping off the press that the Army was standing by for riot duty. Finally I decided it was better that the people hear about it from us, beforehand, than to have the troops show up as a surprise or, worse still, have some enterprising snoop like Ryan find out about them in spite of us. The President had agreed with my views and let the balloon float out into the public airways.

"There is also a rumor," the TV commentator went

on, "completely unconfirmed, that the President himself will address the demonstrators later this evening. As I say, this rumor is completely unconfirmed . . ."

That was news to me. Watching the gathering crowd on the TV screen, I didn't think they looked particularly dangerous. But I knew that in a throng as big as that, a riot could erupt as easily as spitting on somebody's sandal. And a crowd that size would need tanks and water cannon before they were calmed down. *Or maybe worse.*

So I picked listlessly at my dinner, drank damned near a whole bottle of white wine, and watched the special coverage of the demonstration that came on after the regular news show. The speakers were dull, inane, making absurd demands that, if met, would turn the economic clock back a generation and throw *everybody* out of work.

But the people cheered every asinine punchline and waved their signs: COMPUTERS MUST GO! HUMAN DIGNITY REQUIRES HUMAN JOBS. I couldn't see anything dignified about being a secretary or a copyboy or even a typesetter, for that matter. On the other hand, I had a job that exercised my brain, not my hands and legs, so who the hell was I to complain?

It was a combination of the wine and the moronic speeches droning from the TV that put me to sleep. It was the phone's insistent buzzing that woke me up.

I blinked. The TV was still on, and both in the panoramic view of the Capitol showing on the screen and through my own living room windows, I could see that it was dark outside. Night, as they say, had fallen.

The TV audio was saying, "And now, the President of the United States." The view zoomed down to a makeshift podium that had been set up on the Capitol steps. And there he was, James J. Halliday, smiling confidently at the assembled multitudes.

"I don't have a prepared speech," he said disarmingly. "I thought I'd come out here and listen to what *you* have to say."

They roared their approval. *Must be John,* I thought. *He's the charmer.*

The phone was still buzzing, louder and more insistent. I reached over from my chair and tapped the ON button.

On the phone's picture screen, the features of James J. Halliday took form.

"Good evening, Meric," said the President.

I glanced from the phone to the TV, where the President was saying, "I understand that automation has taken many jobs, but that's just a short-term situation . . ."

"Good evening," I said to the phone image. "Your brother's out there walking on water."

"That's Johnny for you," said the President. "He loves it."

"You don't?"

"I'm not much for crowds. I've always preferred Hamilton to Jefferson."

I squinted hard at the phone screen. The wine was making my head thunder.

"It won't do you any good to try to figure out which one I am. You can't tell by looking, and I'm not going to spell it out for you."

"Why'd you call?" I asked.

The President said, "I wanted to make one final appeal to you to call off this ridiculous press conference tomorrow afternoon."

"No deal," I said.

His face hardened. "You'll never get to it. You understand that?"

"Doesn't matter. The story will pop."

With just a hint of exasperation, "You still don't seem to understand, Meric, the power in my hands. By tomorrow afternoon those tapes you mailed out will be destroyed. The people who've been working with you will be silenced. It won't work, Meric. It's doomed."

"Then why call me?"

"Because I'm not a willful slaughterer. I don't want to kill anyone . . ."

"Tell that to your deceased brethren. Tell it to the General, I'm sure he'll understand."

"Meric! Don't force me to act."

"Mr. President . . . this nation has survived an awful lot of stupidity in the White House. We've had ignoramuses for Presidents, we've had innocent do-gooders and out-and-out crooks. But I'm not going to willingly allow a madman to take the job."

"You're a fool, Albano."

"I know it. And I'm scared shitless. I don't want to die. But I can't step away and let you take over. I literally cannot do it! Understand that? Even if I wanted to, I couldn't. What the hell good would it be to live, if I couldn't live with myself?"

"We've already got Ms. Clark," he said flatly. "And Solomon's . . ."

I didn't hear the rest. I felt as if I'd been quick-frozen into solid ice. From somewhere far away, I heard my own voice, grim and tight, whisper, "No deal. It doesn't matter. No deal." And I hated myself for saying it.

I've never seen James J. Halliday's face look so ugly. "All right, Albano. You won't make it through the night."

The phone screen went blank. I clicked it off. On the TV, James J. Halliday was saying:

"That's what the Presidency is for—to listen to the problems of the whole nation, not just one section or one state, and then to take actions that will solve those problems."

They had Vickie. And I wouldn't, *couldn't,* make a trade for her. I don't know how long I sat there, trying to rationalize it. But the simple truth was that Vickie wasn't as important to me as nailing the Halliday murderer. And my own skin.

I realized that my apartment was no longer safe. Especially with Hank gone. But where the hell was there safety? My eyes fixed on the TV screen again.

That vast crowd. Out there, they'd never be able to get to me. I could blend in and disappear.

And besides, I thought, *that's James John out there. If I can get to him and stick with him for the next eighteen hours, we might both make it out of this alive.*

CHAPTER SEVENTEEN

But first I had to get out of my apartment alive. I peeked through the window shutters and saw people walking along the street outside, and the usual solid line of parked cars. Could be an army of hired assassins out there. And I didn't have a car; I'd have to get the door guards to call a taxi for me.

I paced the living room fretfully for a few minutes, certain that I couldn't stay in the apartment, scared at the thought of stepping out into the open, trying not to think about Vickie and what might be happening to her.

Finally I couldn't stand it any longer. I went out into the corridor, after a careful peek from my door, took the emergency stairs two flights *up*, walked all the way across the building to the elevators on that side, and rode down to the laundry room. The garage was one more level down, and if anybody was waiting for me, he'd at least have a scout down there. And out in the lobby.

Tiptoeing back to the delivery ramp behind the laundry room, I looked out into the night-shadowed driveway where the trucks pulled up. There was a gray minibus parked out there, with two men sitting in the cab.

Good Christ, I thought, *they really are out there waiting for me!*

I hurried down to the laundry room. Alex, one of the night security guards, was whistling down the hall toward the guards' locker room.

"Hi, Mr. Albano," he said cheerfully. "Washin' somebody's dirty laundry?" He laughed uproariously at his own joke; he knew my job, and knew that I could take a kidding.

"What're you doing down here?" I asked.

"Gotta take a leak. Hey, you been watchin' those protesters on TV? That's a helluva crowd they got out there. Your boss is talkin' to 'em."

"I know." Then the sudden inspiration came. "Alex . . . do you have a spare uniform in the locker room I could borrow?"

"Huh?"

Thank God he had a sense of humor. I told him it was a joke, and paid him fifty bucks for his extra cap and jacket, and the loan of his car. I promised to leave it at the cab stand three blocks down the avenue.

"Will you take care of the ticket I get when the Pee Dees spot it at the cab stand?"

"Sure."

He trusted me. And my fifty dollars. So, with my heart hammering, I drove slowly out of the garage, wearing the guard's cap and jacket.

Sure enough, there was a blocky-looking character at the exit gate.

The lights weren't all that brilliant down in the garage, although the area around the exit gate was lit better than I would have wished for. The man, whoever he was, kept the gate's bar down so that I couldn't pass through. He stared hard at me.

"Where you going?"

I tried to imitate Alex's accent as best I could. "Gotta get Mr. Kent's pree-scription." And I made a booze-swilling motion that helped to hide my face.

He grinned and reached into the gate booth. The bar swung up and I drove out onto the avenue, very careful not to squeal the tires. I parked at the cab stand, left the cap and jacket on the front seat of the car, and took one of the cabs.

"You ain't supposed to park there," the cabbie said as I opened the rear door.

I ducked inside. "It's a joke I'm playing on a friend," I said.

His black face, staring back at me in the mirror, wasn't at all amused. "Some joke," he grunted.

The crowd around the Capitol was so huge that the traffic cops wouldn't let us get within five blocks of the Hill. Or stop. They kept waving us on, until we were detoured down Virginia Avenue, halfway to the god-damned Navy Yard. The driver fumed and grumbled up front while I fumed and fretted in the darkness of the back seat.

He wormed through endless lines of parked buses up along Sixth Street Southeast and got as close as the Library of Congress Annex. The police had sawhorses and fire trucks blocking off the streets beyond there.

"Close as I can get," the driver said.

I gave him a five, "It'll do." I felt a little annoyed that he didn't even go through the pretense of trying to make change.

I walked through the soft night air past an empty fire truck, toward the library's main building a couple of blocks away. There wasn't much of a crowd down here, but there were lots of people milling around, clustered in little groups on the corners, sitting on the curbs. Young people mostly, kids, black and white mixed. Normally, in this particular neighborhood, the streets are abandoned after dark. Too dangerous. But not tonight. These out-of-towners were strong enough in numbers to provide their own safety.

Their older peers were out in front of the Capitol, peaceably assembled—as the First Amendment puts it—to seek redress of grievances. These kids had just come along for the ride. And to be thrown in the front lines by their elders if it looked like a clash with the police or Army was coming up.

But the President was taking the venom out of the throng. There'd be no bloody confrontation; he'd turned it into a question-and-answer session, air your gripes, come to me all ye who labor and are hard pressed. He was good at it. James John, that is. Back at the White House was that other one, the one who'd phoned me, the one who had Vickie and was going to try to kill Johnny. And me.

I got a couple of odd looks from the kids as I purposefully walked toward the library's main building. I obviously wasn't one of them. Wrong uniform: business slacks and shirtjac instead of glitterpants and vest. Wrong age. Wrong attitude. But they didn't bother me.

The guard at the library's side entrance did. He was in *his* uniform: plastic armor, riot helmet with visor pulled down to shield his face, bandoleer of gas grenades, dartgun, electric prod, heavy boots.

"The building is closed, sir," he said, very politely and steel hard.

I pulled rank. Dug out my ID and said, "I've got to get to the President, and the crowd's too thick up front of the Capitol. Thought I'd go through the slideway tunnel."

He bucked me upstairs. Called his sergeant on his helmet radio. The police sergeant came up and offered to provide me with an escort to get me through the crowd in front of the President. I declined. "Don't want to make that much of a disturbance in front of The Man," I said. Actually, I didn't want to call that much attention to myself. I might be a clay pigeon, but there was no sense painting myself dayglo orange.

The sergeant called a captain who finally relented and personally escorted me into the library, down to the connecting tunnel, and along the rubbery moving belt that slid us both to the Capitol building. Secret Service men were prowling around the slideway's terminal area, and I had to show my ID again and go through a security arch to prove who—and how unarmed—I was.

The guy in charge of the security detail looked so much like McMurtrie that I wondered if they had cloned Secret Service men, too. He took me in tow and waved the police captain back to his post.

"The Capitol building is sealed shut against visitors," he said as we rode the elevator up to the main rotunda.

"Good," I said, wondering if this guy knew that there was a brigade of men just like him who were looking for me.

"The President didn't inform us that he expected his press secretary to meet him here," he said suspiciously.

"It's a hectic evening. None of us has planned much of this in advance."

He accepted that, although it was clear he didn't like it. Unplanned events such as sudden decisions to address large crowds informally, and having visitors like the press secretary drop into a cleared area, made him unhappy. Good. That meant he wasn't in on the plan to get me. I hoped.

We stepped out of the elevator into the vast, empty, echoing rotunda, our footsteps clicking hollowly on the floor. It was only partially lit; you could see your way across the floor all right, and up in the dome, Brumidi's blasphemous painting—turning Washington into a small-time rococo Italian saint—was all too visible. But the galleries that ringed the dome, several tiers up, were darkened.

"I'll have to ask you to stay in the rotunda area," the security man told me. "We've sealed off the rest of the building. The President will come back here when he's finished speaking to the crowd."

I nodded, just as the crowd gave a cheering roar. It sounded almost like booming surf inside the rotunda.

Although the main expanse of the rotunda's floor was empty, there were knots of well-tailored men and women at every corridor leading out. It felt a little eerie, having the whole damned place to myself, with no tourists clicking their cameras, no troops of Scouts goggle-eyeing their way around, nobody bumping into you, no tour guides talking about marble or historic events or the problems of painting the inside of the dome so that the picture showed proper perspective from the floor.

I glanced up at Old George. He looked kind of uncomfortable up there in rococo heaven. I felt damned uncomfortable down here on the modern earth. And exposed. This wasn't what I had planned on at all.

And then I noticed that I wasn't alone. Sitting on a bench near the bronze of crusty old Andy Jackson was General Halliday. Alone.

I went to him.

"What're you doing here?" he asked, without preliminaries.

"Hiding." I sat down beside him.

He gave me a sour look.

"One of your boys is out to get me."

"You've got a hell of an imagination."

"He phoned me this evening. Said they've taken my assistant prisoner. There was a goon squad waiting for me at my apartment building."

The General shook his head disbelievingly.

"If you're lucky," I said, the heat rising in me, "you could get to see a real Western-style shootout right here in the rotunda. His goon squad against John's security force. Maybe we ought to buy score cards . . ."

"Don't be an idiot, Albano," the General said. "If he wants to nail you, he won't do it that way."

"Whose side are you on?" I asked him.

He just looked at me.

"You know which of them is killing the others. Do you want to let him succeed or stop him? Or are you content to let 'survival of the fittest' be the rule, and go along with whoever's left?"

His expression didn't change or soften in the slightest. But his voice sank to a whisper. "I wish to hell I knew what to do."

"If I make it through the night, I'm going to give the whole story to the press," I said. "Tomorrow."

"Then my guess is that you won't make it through the night."

"That's why I want to stick close to John."

"Why him?"

"He was talking with the crowd when his brother called me. So it can't be him."

General Halliday said nothing.

"And I don't think it could be Joshua," I went on. "He didn't strike me as having the balls for this kind of thing. So it must be either Jeffrey or Jackson."

"Brilliant deduction. But which one?"

"The one who phoned me earlier this evening."

"How much earlier?"

I shrugged. "Let's see . . ."

The General hunched forward on the wooden bench. "Jackson's been here for the past two hours. He and I came together, right behind Johnny."

"How the hell did you get past everybody?"

He grinned, and his face folded into a relief map of wrinkles. "A phony mustache and beard, pair of tinted glasses. We came in with my own security men. Those Secret Service kids never tumbled."

"Where is he now?"

"Up in the galleries somewhere, watching his brother, I expect."

My mind was racing. "And he's been here two hours? All that time? Here? With you?"

The General nodded.

"Then if he's been here with you, and John's been outside talking with the crowd . . . and we agree that Joshua's not the one . . . then it's got to be Jeffrey. He's the only one who could have phoned me from the White House."

The General stared down at the floor, silent.

Jeffrey, I thought. *The expert in defense policy. The one I flew back from Aspen with. He's the murderer.*

"You're sure it's Jackson you came here with?"

"I know my own boys," the General said flatly.

I got up from the bench. "I want to see him. Now."

The General pointed skyward. "He's up there in one of the galleries."

I strained my eyes, searching the darkened galleries that ringed the dome's interior. Nothing . . . wait. A shadowy figure. A motion past one of the tall windows. I headed for the nearest staircase.

The stairs had been closed to the public for years. Too steep and narrow for large crowds of tourists. A century ago, visitors had become shitty enough to toss their garbage over the railings just to see who got splatted down on the floor. So the galleries were closed to visitors.

I was intercepted by the inevitable Secret Service agent, of course. A hard-faced woman this time. When I showed her who I was and told her I was going upstairs, and explained that it was impossible to leave the dome from those galleries, she relented. After a radio check with her boss.

The marble stairs are steep and strange in the dark. Half a flight, then a level stretch, then six more steps, then another flat, and then a long flight of narrow stairs, with your feet clacking and making weird, shifting echoes as you go along. The light from the dome was filtered by flimsy-looking metal railings in places, blocked out entirely by solid walls elsewhere, so the going was slow and groping.

I was puffing by the time I reached the first gallery. I thought that was where I'd seen Jackson, but he wasn't anywhere in sight. Footsteps echoed somewhere; it was impossible to get a fix on the direction of sounds up here. The echoes floated ghostlike in the still air. I went to the marble balustrade and looked down. Couldn't see the General from here. The floor of the rotunda looked empty and damned far away. A long way to fall.

I hustled all around the gallery, stopping every now and then to call out, "Jackson!" and get nothing in return except the goddamnedest syncopation of echoes you ever heard. *Why the hell's he playing hide and seek?*

So up to the next level I went, stumbling, tripping over the even narrower, steeper steps, cursing the darkness without a flashlight. Once I grabbed at one of the metal railings. It shook in my hand. Not much protection there. Up I went.

Halfway to the topmost gallery I paused to catch my breath. And heard somebody else's footsteps again. Slow, measured, patient, steady. *Clack ... clack ... clack ... clack.* The echoes surrounded me. They could have been coming from above me, behind me, right beside me, and I'd never know it. But deep inside my scary guts, I got the firm feeling that they were coming up the stairs from behind me. I was being followed.

I pushed myself up the final sets of stairs to the top gallery. Puffing, leaning on the balustrade, and staring down at the hard, hard floor a hundred feet below, I realized that the echoing footsteps had also stopped. But before I could try to figure out what that meant, I heard something else. So faint I couldn't really tell what it was. Breathing. Or maybe the softest kind of a low chuckling laugh.

I looked around the shadowed gallery. Across the dome's open space, on the other side, the half-hidden figure of a man in a light-colored suit stepped out of the darkness and up to the marble balustrade. I couldn't see his face; it was in shadows. But I knew that figure. It was one of the brothers. He beckoned to me, waving with one hand.

Like the helpless ingénue in a Gothic nightmare, I started around the gallery toward him. Something in my head was screaming a warning of danger at me, but my body obediently followed The Man's summons.

As soon as I started moving, the *clack ... clack* of the other person's footsteps started again.

I paused briefly at one of the narrow, round-topped windows and looked out toward the West Front. The crowd was still there, quiet now, a mass of solidly packed people that covered the western side of the Hill and spilled out across Union Square and around the New Reflecting Pool. Faintly, faintly, I heard the voice of James J. Halliday, electronically amplified, still talking to them. John had been out there for more than two hours now, and was still going strong. Great copy for tonight's news shows and tomorrow's papers. The stuff of legends: President meets people, face to face, heart to heart.

I prayed to God and anybody else who'd listen that John would be alive tomorrow to see those headlines. And Vickie. And me.

The echoes of those following footsteps stirred me out of reverie. I looked across the dome again, and he was still standing there, a little deeper back in the shadows now, so that he couldn't be seen from the floor. But I could see him. I hurried across the gallery to him.

"Jackson?" My whisper bounced crazily and shattered into a million echoes.

"Yes," he whispered back, and the sound seemed to come from everywhere.

I got up close enough to see that he was still wearing the phony mustache and beard. They helped to make his face disappear into the shadows. As I stepped toward him, he slowly pulled them off and stuffed them into the pocket of his mandarin-style tunic. His teeth flashed white in a big grin.

"Someone's following me," I said.

"I know."

I looked down that deep, dizzying well of emptiness and saw that the bench near Old Hickory's statue was unoccupied. There was nobody down on the rotunda floor at all. Even the Secret Service guards seemed to have melted away.

"Why would . . . ?"

Jackson gave me the famous Halliday smile. "This involves more than you and me, Meric."

"But those stairs are awfully tough for a man his age. . . . I damned near collapsed on them."

"You mean the General?"

Clack . . . clack . . . clack . . . clack. The steps were slow but doggedly steady.

"Yes, the General . . . who else?"

Jackson said nothing. I tried to fathom the expression on his face, but it was too dark to see him that well. He was grinning, that much I could tell.

For some reason my mouth kept making conversation while those clacking steps drew nearer.

"This whole idea of cloning," I said. "It seems awfully . . . *planned*. You guys were practically programmed to become President, weren't you?"

"We didn't lead the carefree lives of your average American boy." Jackson said it evenly. No humor in it. No bitterness.

"It's all terribly cold-blooded. I mean, you and your brothers being deliberately trained like that from infancy."

"Cold-blooded," Jackson said emotionlessly. "You don't know the half of it."

"No, I guess I don't."

"There's nothing wrong with planning," he said. "Nothing wrong with setting your sights on a goal and then doing everything you can to attain it. That's how this continent got discovered, you know. That's how we gained our independence. Move heaven and earth to reach your goal. Pike's Peak or bust. I shall return. That's one small step for a man, one giant leap for mankind."

"You're a historian?" I tried to make it sound light, but those footsteps echoing behind me gave my voice a hollow ring.

"Every President becomes a historian, Meric. You soak in history once you're in the White House. And what's the basic lesson of history? The goal justifies the means. If you win."

If you win . . . if you win . . . echoed eerily around the gallery.

"History's written by the winners," Jackson said. "Fix your sights on your goal and stop at nothing to reach it. That's what makes history. Columbus. Old Sam Adams and his Minutemen. The Forty-Niners. MacArthur. Armstrong. Truman. The Kennedys. They all did it that way. And me. That's the way I'm doing it. It's the only way it can be done."

My heart turned to ice.

"You *are* Jackson?" I asked.

His smile returned. "Yes. I'm Jackson. Don't be afraid. I am the President."

Somehow that didn't reassure me at all.

Jackson turned his head ever so slightly, looked past my shoulder. I turned. Instead of the ramrod-stiff figure of the General that I expected, it was Laura. Dressed in white. Like a bride. Or a mourner from some ancient tribe.

"Those stairs," she said breathlessly as she approached us. "They're killers." Her eyes were bright, gleaming.

Jackson nodded. "Tourists used to collapse on the stairs. That's why these galleries were closed to the public."

Laura looked straight at me but didn't say a word. It was as if she were looking through me, as if I no longer existed for her. She stepped over to the stone niche where the window was set and sat on its sill.

"You didn't have to come," Jackson said. "I told you I could handle this by myself."

Laura smiled at him. "I just wanted to be sure, darling. I wanted to see it for myself." Her eyes glittered as if she were on a drug trip. And I knew which drug it was: power.

"This is more than a family matter," I said. "Unless you're thinking of the whole population of the United States as your family."

"Don't be silly, Meric." It was her first acknowledgment of my presence.

"We've got to stop these murders," I said. "And Jeffrey's snatched Vickie Clark, and . . ."

"You're sure it's Jeffrey?" Jackson asked.

"I explained it to the General, downstairs. John's outside with the crowd, right?"

Jackson nodded.

"You're both certain it's John out there?"

Laura said, "Of course it's John. None of the others could handle a crowd like that. John's the face, the public figure, the candidate and handshaker. He enjoys crowds."

The man whose hand I shook, I remembered.

"And we're agreed it can't be Joshua."

"Josh couldn't . . ."

Laura fidgeted with the little purse she was holding on her lap. "Do get on with it."

"You're absolutely certain Jeffrey's the right one?" Jackson asked me.

"Yes."

"Why?"

"Because he called me this evening and threatened to kill Vickie and me both if I don't call off my press conference tomorrow."

Jackson looked at me curiously. "How do you know it was Jeffrey?"

"It had to be. John was already speaking here. We agree it can't be Joshua. You were here with the General. . . ."

"They have phones here," Jackson said.

I stopped with my mouth still open.

"But . . . your father said . . . the General told me he was with you all night."

"That's right, he was," Jackson said.

"Just as he is now," Laura added. "Down there."

I suddenly understood how a mouse feels when it is cornered by a pair of cats: very small, very alone, and scared mindless.

"Y . . . You're the one who called me?"

"That's right, Meric. Tonight I finish the task I started eighteen months ago. Tomorrow morning I will be the sole occupant of the Oval Office. I will be the President, alone and entirely."

I turned to Laura. "And you're going to let him?"

"Of course."

"For God's sake, Laura—stop him!"

"Why? So John can go on making pretty faces to the public and compromising with every beggar who comes in off the street? Or Josh can stay in hiding all the time? Or Jeff can keep on playing soldier? Jackson's been the only real man in this whole family. I've known that for years. Jackson's the strong one. It's survival of the fittest."

"But he's killing his brothers!" My voice was a mousy squeak. I could barely hear it myself.

"The President's got to be *strong*." Laura's voice practically purred. Her eyes were afire now.

"But he's a murderer!"

Jackson snapped, "Name one President who wasn't. Truman? Lincoln? Either Roosevelt? Nixon? Brown? They all had blood on their hands."

"Sweet Jesus, the two of you are insane."

"Meric," Jackson said, in that *tone,* that *inflection,* that I'd heard a thousand times in the White House.

I stared at him.

"We've been very patient with you, Meric. I've given you every opportunity to stop opposing me. Even Laura has tried to make you see . . ."

"Tried to buy me off, you mean."

"You had your chance," Laura said.

I started to shake my head.

Jackson said, "There's no other way, Meric. We'll have to do away with you. And Ms. Clark, too."

"Like you killed the others?"

"No . . ." He fumbled in his tunic pocket and pulled out a small plastic syringe. "No, you're not going to die of immunological breakdown. That would raise too many questions. And, incidentally, I got the virus from the University of Pennsylvania's biochemistry labs. They have very lax security systems at universities, you know. A Government man can go anywhere and see anything he wants to. The professors all trail him with their tongues hanging out, hoping to lap up some droppings of Federal grant money."

"How'd you know?"

"Don't be naive. I didn't do it personally. I'm an economist, not a biochemist."

I turned back toward Laura. "You're going to let him do it?"

She pulled a small handgun from her purse. "I'm going to help him."

"It'll be hard to explain a gunshot wound."

"This doesn't shoot bullets," she replied. "Tranquilizer darts. They make the same puncture as a doctor's needle."

"You're going to die of a fatal heart attack," Jackson said, holding the syringe up beside his face. "The stairs were too much for you. You're really not in good physical shape. All the excitement of the President's impromptu meeting with the Neo-Luddites outside the Capitol . . . too much for the press secretary's heart."

"The day I die," I said as evenly as I could, "my whole story gets published. Not only here, but overseas as well."

"Wrong," Jackson said. "We've already intercepted the two tapes you sent overseas. They've been destroyed."

"I don't believe you!" But I really did. Why else would they feel free to knock me off?

"And we have a good idea of where the third tape went," he added. "The publisher of the *Globe* likes to think he's a friend of Presidents. I'll get the tape before any of your old cronies listen to it."

I started to reply, but clamped my mouth shut instead.

"That leaves only your erstwhile bodyguard," Jackson said, "who seems to have run off to parts unknown."

"Nope. I'm right here."

Hank Solomon's voice!

"Y'all jes' better line up along th' railin' there and put yer assorted instruments down on th' top of it."

Jackson spun around fiercely and tried to find the source of the disembodied voice. Hank's twang echoed through the shadows. He might have been anywhere. Laura jumped to her feet and also peered into the darkness.

"Now lissen," Hank said, "I got a regulation 7.6-millimeter pistol in mah hand. Nothin' fancy. It makes a lotta noise, and it puts a big ol' hole in yew. It'll make a mess outta yer pretty white dress, ma'am. So put them instruments *down.* Y'hear?"

But Laura, instead of giving up, grabbed me by the collar and jammed her gun to my head. "I'll kill him!" she shouted, and her voice shrilled off every corner and curve of the stonework around us.

I reacted without thinking. Instead of being scared, I was damned sore. I shoved Laura away from me and turned toward Jackson. Something went *pop* and I felt a sting in the back of my neck.

Jackson pushed past me and ran clattering along the gallery, heading for the stairs. I saw Laura glaring pure hatred at me. I took a step toward her, but my feet wouldn't work right. I stumbled. She cracked me in the face with her goddamned popgun and down I went.

The marble was cold.

Somebody turned me over on my back. Hank grinned down at me. "Y'all got a buzzful of trank in yew, boy."

"Get them," I mumbled, feeling like my head was numb with Novocain. "Why dintcha shoot him?"

"Eighty Secret Service agents down there and yew want me t' take a shot at the President?"

"You've got to . . ." I tried to get my legs working, tried to get to my feet.

"Stay there," Hank commanded. "I'll get him."

He disappeared while I was still doing an imitation of a beached flounder. The echoes! I heard feet running on marble as if they were racing in circles inside my head. Hard breathing. Whispers. Coughs.

I finally struggled to my feet and grabbed the balustrade. Leaning over it like a seasick tourist, I tried to peer into the gloomy shadows to find out what was happening. Couldn't see a damned thing. And it was all wavering in front of my eyes, lurching up and down and sideways. Damned if I wasn't seasick.

I looked down to the floor of the rotunda. A *long* way down. Tiny little people were slowly gathering down there, their heads craned upward. They had heard the sounds of a struggle coming from some-where.

A shout. A pair of voices cursing. Then a body crashed through one of those flimsy railings, screaming all the way down to the floor. It hit with a solid *thunk* that ended its screaming forever. The body was wear-ing a light-colored mandarin suit. I threw up.

I must have passed out. The next thing I knew, Hank was bending over me, his face very solemn. "I got him," he said simply. Then he helped me to my feet and we staggered downward, on those dark narrow stairways, toward the floor of the rotunda.

I heard the pounding of an army rushing up the stairs toward us. It turned out to be only a dozen or so Secret Service men. They looked grim, angry, puzzled, all at the same time. We passed the broken railing, and I glanced out toward the floor. A crowd of agents was surrounding the body. From this high I could see that Jackson's fake mustache and beard had floated out of his pocket and landed almost on top of his grotesquely twisted body.

The agents with us didn't ask any questions. They didn't say a word. It was damned eerie. Silently they escorted us down to the floor.

Across the way, beside the huge Columbus Portal, stood the General, flanked by two agents. He looked old and bent. But when he saw us, he straightened.

"He killed my son!" he shouted, and suddenly grabbed the gun from the shoulder holster of the agent on his left.

Hank pushed me to the floor as the General fired. A long ugly gouge ripped up the floor inches from my face. I heard Hank's gun go off, deafening, right in my ears. The General crumpled.

I looked up at Hank. He was smiling.

"That's the one I was after. He's the sumbitch that killed McMurtrie."

CHAPTER EIGHTEEN

I woke up in a hospital room.

It was spinning around in circles, slowly, and refused to stop. I squeezed my eyes shut and then cautiously opened them again. Still circles. I didn't remember being brought here. Didn't remember a damned thing, in fact, since Hank had killed the General. Just his grim, death's head smile as he let his gun drop to the floor and all the Secret Service agents in the world rushed him.

Gradually the room settled down. I expected to feel a monumental headache, but I didn't. I felt foggy, but without pain. Kind of stiff, heavy-limbed. It was a real effort to lift my head and squint at the brightness outside the room's one window.

Looked like midday out there. Maybe afternoon. I could see the double-tiered roadway of the Route 495 Beltway, and a forest of radio-TV antennas off among the checkerboard of neat little suburban houses that covered the once-green and rolling hills. *Walter Reed,* I realized. *They've stashed me at Walter Reed Hospital.*

Even if I'd felt strong enough to get up, I knew the door would be locked, and an armed soldier or two would be on the other side of it. Maybe Marines, in their flashy dress uniforms and their *they shall not pass* faces, with those neat little automatic pistols on their hips, the kind that can clean out a room in twelve seconds flat.

I wondered for a long while what had happened to

Hank. And Vickie. And those tapes I'd sent overseas. And Johnny Harrison. I began to try to figure out how I could get word to Len Ryan about everything that had happened. It was quite a surprise when I looked out the window again and it was dark outside. I must have fallen asleep in the middle of my intense thinking.

A sweet-faced black nurse came in, all serious business in stiff white uniform and no chitchat with the patient. She raised my bed without asking me if I wanted it that way, looking as if she were afraid to exchange words with me.

"Will I live?" I asked.

She almost smiled, then caught herself. "The monitors are all in the green."

The bed was loaded with sensors, she meant, and my temperature, heart rate, breathing, and everything else—including conversation—was being monitored automatically at the nurses' station somewhere outside the room.

Will I live? I asked myself. A subtler question than that nurse knew.

She left the room momentarily and came back with a tray of food. To my surprise, I was really hungry. I went through the chicken dinner in record time. Even demolished the pasty-looking bread slices. No wine. Just milk and coffee. I drank them both.

The nurse took the tray and left. I remained sitting up in the bed, with no way to crank the damned thing down again. Not that I wanted to. I was feeling okay now. For the first time, I studied the room I was in. Not much to see. One chair, a bureau made of walnut veneer, pastel green walls, a mirror—I looked seedy, needed a shave, but otherwise unhaggard—one window, a doorless closet in which hung the clothes I'd come in with, and the door to the corridor outside.

Which opened, just about then, to admit the President.

Somehow I wasn't surprised. He looked drawn, strained. Must've been one helluva day for him.

He reached for the room's only chair as the door clicked firmly shut behind him. I had a chance to glimpse the corridor. There *were* soldiers out there. Armed.

The President sat down like an old man, slowly, painfully. He looked as if he hadn't slept for a long time.

"My father's dead," he said wearily.

"It was self-defense," I answered. "I saw it. He shot at Hank and . . ."

"He shot at *you*, Meric. He was trying to shut you up once and for all. Solomon killed him to get even for McMurtrie. Half the agents there were McMurtrie's friends. They damned near pinned a medal on Solomon."

I thought about it for a moment. "Guess I missed today's press briefing."

"I guess you did. Hunter handled it."

"How'd he explain . . . ?"

"He didn't. He said you'd collapsed at your desk and had been taken to Walter Reed Hospital. Most of the press corps seemed surprised but not suspicious. One of them . . . a new man, from Boston . . ."

"Len Ryan?"

The President nodded. "He wanted to interview you here in the hospital. We let him see you this afternoon, while you were asleep. That seemed to satisfy him."

"He wanted to make sure I was alive."

"Apparently."

"Sir," I asked, "you are John, aren't you?"

"Yes. There are only three of us left. It's getting easier to guess, isn't it?" He smiled, but it was the kind of smile a soldier makes after a battle, when he's come through it alive but most of his buddies haven't.

"Hunter didn't tell them anything about last night?"

"Two nights ago. It was two nights ago that it all happened."

"I've been conked out that long?"

"You took a powerful dose of tranquilizer."

"But nothing was said to the press?"

"No. Not a thing. My father's going to officially die of a heart attack in Aspen in a few days. Robert is out there now, getting things arranged. Laura ..." He stopped, and for an instant I thought his control was finally going to break. But he went on, "Laura is going on a round-the-world trip. Under heavy guard. We agreed to keep her out of it, to keep the marriage going for the rest of my term. It won't be the first White House marriage between enemies."

"You're going to try to cover up the whole story?"

His eyes flashed. "Try to?"

"You can't keep it quiet forever."

"For God's sake, Meric, haven't you had enough?" His voice rose. It didn't get louder, but it got an edge of steel to it. An edge that could cut.

"What do you ..."

"Four of us killed. My father. He may not have been the closest father a man ever had, but he's dead. My wife. Because of you."

"I didn't ..."

"You didn't pull the trigger, but if you'd kept your damned mouth shut none of this would have happened."

"And *you'd* be dead."

"Maybe."

"And Jackson would be on the throne."

"It's not a throne."

"It would be, once he got his hands on it. He was insane, sir. Crazy. Power-mad."

"He was my brother!"

"He would've killed you in a hot second! He killed three of your brothers. You were going to get yours right there in the Capitol. He told me so."

He glared at me, teeth bared, hating the whole ugly business and hating me because of it.

"It's true, sir. He would've killed you and taken over the Presidency and turned this nation into his own private dictatorship."

"He couldn't have gotten away with that."

"He would've tried. He would've demolished everything you've been trying to accomplish. And you know damned well there are plenty of people around this town who would've gladly helped him do it. Including your father."

The President looked away from me. He pushed himself up from the chair and went to the window.

After several minutes of silence, he said, very low, "You're right. I know you're right. But it still doesn't go down very easily."

"I don't see how it could."

He turned back toward me. "All right. It's all over with. Finished. The ship of state has weathered another storm. The problem is, what do we do next? There are still some odds and ends to clean up."

"Where are Vickie and Hank?"

"Solomon is in protective custody over at the FBI Center. They've pumped him full of truth drugs and wrung him dry, but otherwise he's unhurt."

"And Vickie?"

"She's being held in one of the Federal housing developments in Anacostia. She has a very nice apartment and two friendly women security guards to see to it that she's comfortable. Apparently she's quite anxious to find out what happened to you."

I let out a sigh of relief that I hadn't known was in me.

"That brings it all down to you, Meric," the President said.

"What do you mean?"

He spread his hands in a gesture somewhere between disgust and helplessness. "I can put Hank Solomon in a bottle and make certain he never bothers me. I can see to it that Ms. Clark is bought off, or moved out of the way . . ."

"You'd better not . . ."

"Listen to me," he said, and it was a command. He pulled the chair around backwards and sat on it again. "My real problem is you and your damned Boston conscience. Are you going to keep quiet about this business or aren't you? I can handle the others, but only if you stay shut."

He folded his arms on the back of the chair and rested his chin on them. He was smiling! He was enjoying this ... this game, this deadly round of give-and-take. It was the kind of thing he'd been born—no, raised—to do. The battle of wills. The old political infighting: I'll give you this if you'll give me that.

I looked at him for a long, long time. Seemed like years. Must have been a few minutes, at least.

"Well?" he asked. "I want your promise of silence. Everything is settled now, except for you. It all depends on you, Meric."

"No, Mr. President," I finally said. "It all depends on *you*."

His chin lifted. "What do you mean?"

"You've got to tell them."

"Them? The press?"

"The people. You've got to tell them the whole thing."

"Never!"

"You've got to tell them there's more than one of you, at least," I said. "Use your father's death as an excuse, if you want to. But you can't go on with a committee in the White House. Not unless the people know about it and approve."

"That's impossible. No way."

I felt my own voice getting stronger. "The people didn't elect a gang of brothers. They elected one man. You. You're the only one they saw; you're the one who made the speeches and did the campaigning."

"But I was using the expertise of my brothers," the President said. "They put the ideas into the speeches. They worked out the problems and the solutions."

"Tell the people," I urged. "You'll never be able to keep this thing covered up now, anyway. Too many people know about it. It's going to leak sooner or later. For God's sake ... go to the people and tell them!"

"They'll want me to resign," he said.

"Maybe."

"Can you picture this country with Lazar as President?" he demanded. "It'd be a catastrophe."

I answered, "Can you picture what Lazar will do when he finds out what's been going on? I won't tell him, but you know damned well somebody will. You can't keep this quiet forever."

"You think not?" And I saw some of Jackson's power lust glint in his eyes.

"I think not," I said. "The story will leak out. It's too big to keep covered. If it doesn't come out now, it certainly will in the next election campaign."

He nodded grimly. "During the primaries."

"Sir," I said, "even Lazar as President would be better than a man the people couldn't trust. Maybe you could call for a national referendum . . . a vote of confidence. Then if it goes against you, *both* you and Lazar resign and call for a special election."

"That's crazy. Nobody would go for that."

"The people would."

"I mean nobody here in Washington."

"But the *people* would. It's their Government, you know."

"Stop mouthing sermons. This is politics. This is real."

I took a deep breath. "Sir, I honestly think that the only way you can survive in the Presidency is to tell the entire story. Freely. Now. Don't wait for somebody to dig it up and lay the skeletons on your doorstep."

"You're full of shit, Meric. You're so transparent, it's almost funny. You couldn't care less about my surviving in the Presidency—"

"That's not true!"

"The hell it isn't. What's really bugging you is the idea of keeping the Presidency intact. You're not working for me, you're working for the goddamned Constitution."

Meric Albano, the patriot? "No, I'm not that noble," I countered. "But it wouldn't be a bad idea if you and the Constitution were on the same side."

He threw his head back and pleaded with the ceiling. "He doesn't want a President, he wants a saint. A Catholic saint, at that!"

"Only dead men can be made into saints," I said. "I've worked damned hard to keep you alive."

He snapped those deep brown eyes on me. It was like facing a pair of gun muzzles. "I owe you that much, don't I?"

"You don't owe me a thing."

"Not much," he muttered. He got up from the chair again and started pacing the room. Not much floor space for him to work with; three long strides and he was at the window, four in the other direction and he reached the door.

Turning back toward me, he said, "I could put a pretty good face on it. Tell the people that my brothers were my advisers . . . the closest kind of aides a President could have. Hell, Kennedy made his brother the Attorney General, didn't he? And there's no hint of scandal; I mean, as far as money or political deals are involved."

"I could help you write a speech like that," I said.

He grinned. "A referendum. It might work out. It could work." The grin broadened. "I can see the Congress wrestling with that one. They'd be on the spot to decide on calling the special election or not." He laughed outright.

I shifted on the bed. "It'll be damned hard to keep that shoot-out in the Capitol rotunda hushed up."

"It can be done," he said. "If I can count on you to keep your mouth shut, I can cover the rest of them with the National Security Act. They'll keep quiet."

"You'll have to tell the people about the cloning," I said.

"Yes. They won't like that. They'll be afraid of it."

"But you're not the one who did it," I pointed out. "It was your father's decision. You were only a helpless infant."

He stared at me for a moment. "There's still hope for you, Meric."

"And you'll have to bring your brothers out to the public," I quickly added.

"H'mm. I'm not sure Josh could take that. He's pretty close to a nervous breakdown as it is."

"It could work," I said.

"You don't really care if it works or not," he accused. But he was still grinning slightly. "All you're interested in is the national welfare."

I shrugged an admission of guilt.

"But I'll bet I could swing it," he said. "I could get them to swallow it. Especially if I start right after my father's funeral. Get their full sympathy."

I sank back in the propped-up bed, watching him plan his campaign in his head. I didn't think he'd have a prayer of keeping his office. It would be too much for the public to accept. But then I hadn't thought the public would elect Brandon, his predecessor. And if he'd tell the public that much of his story, I'd work like hell to help him. He deserved that much from me.

CHAPTER NINETEEN

They let me out of the hospital the next day. The first thing I did was call Vickie. She had just been turned loose, too, so I hopped a taxi to her apartment, intending to take her out to lunch. We had a lot to talk about.

I leaned on her bell and she opened the door immediately.

"You're really okay?" we both asked simultaneously. And then we laughed and we were in each other's arms and there wasn't a damned thing to discuss.

It was getting toward dusk as we lay side by side on her waterbed and Vickie said, "Is it really all over?"

"Yeah. We're setting up a press conference next Monday to . . ."

"I don't mean that," she said. Turning on her side, sending waves through the waterbed and through me, she asked, "Is it over between you and Laura Halliday? The torch is extinguished?"

"How'd you know . . . ?"

"I knew," she said simply. "And I get the feeling that you're finally free of her."

"It was over a long time ago," I said, "only I didn't understand it."

"You're much too good for her," Vickie said.

"For a researcher," I joked, "you're damned perceptive."

"For a reporter," she cracked back, "you're a warm and sensitive human being."

"A credit to your race," I said.

"An ornament to your profession."

"A bird in the hand is worth two in the bush."

"Fifty-four forty or fight."

All of a sudden I was making a confession. "There were a couple of hours back there . . . when Jackson told me he'd picked you up and offered to trade you for my silence . . ."

Vickie closed her eyes. "I know. I did the same thing. They told me they'd let you go if I promised to keep quiet. I didn't promise."

We were both quiet for a while. There wasn't all that much to say. The phone rang.

Vickie sat up, sending a small *tsunami* across the bed, and touched the VOICE ONLY button.

"Hiya." Hank Solomon's voice sounded cheerful. "Y'all busy or are y'all jes restin'?"

How'd he know . . . ? I started to wonder.

But Vickie took it calmly. "Do you want to talk to Meric?"

"Both of y'all. Thought yew might like to come out fer some dinner and hear 'bout mah new promotion."

So we showered and dressed and met Hank at the old Black Angus, where he treated us to real Texas beef steaks and the news that he'd been promoted to head the security detail for Vice-President Lazar.

"Kicked upstairs, t' keep me quiet."

Knowing what the President thought of Lazar, I had to laugh. But still, it was more than fair treatment for the man who'd shot the General. All the other Secret Service agents who'd been present at the Capitol shootout had been transferred out of Washington: the farther the better, apparently. A few had gone to American Samoa. At least one of them was on her way to the lunar station, although why they needed a Secret Service security woman on the moon was a question I never got a satisfactory answer to.

It was a busy week. Not that setting up a major press conference for the President was all that difficult. Hell, if I couldn't do that blindfolded, with the staff and experience at my fingertips, I should look for another line of work.

I put in a lot of time helping the President to write his speech. All three of them contributed ideas and phrasings. Even Joshua seemed to have pulled out of his funk and added some key insights to humanize the prose.

The thing that was really banging away inside my head was Vickie. I kept thinking about her, day and night. I spent all the time I could with her, and wanted to be with her when we were apart. I was scared brainless about big words like love, and even more so of the idea of marriage. But somehow she seemed an integral part of my life now, in a way that Laura or any other woman I'd known had never been.

The morning of the press conference, I couldn't stand it anymore. We were fidgeting around in the State Dining Room, on the first floor of the White House, where the press conference was going to take place in another half-hour. The dining tables and chairs had been removed, a podium for the President had been set up right in front of Healy's portrait of Lincoln, and the big room was crammed with folding chairs for the news people. TV crews were rolling their cameras in and talking into their headsets to the remote transmitting station in the van outside.

I pulled Vickie from the umpteenth shuffling through the piles of copies of the President's speech and dragged her out into the hallway.

"What's the matter?" she asked, looking troubled.

This time I was glad that my mouth worked independently of my brains. Otherwise I could never have uttered a sound.

"Will you marry me?" I blurted.

She looked sort of surprised for an instant, then smiled. "I thought you'd never ask."

I blinked. "You mean you will?"

She had to reach up on tiptoes to peck me swiftly on the lips. "No. Not yet. But I'll move in with you."

I must have looked pretty stupid. I know I felt it.

"That's a beginning," Vickie said. "Marriage is awfully permanent . . . or at least it should be. Let's take it slow."

With a nod, I agreed.

"Besides," she added, with her elfin grin, "my lease is up at the end of the month."

I didn't let her get away with that. I grabbed her and really kissed her.

I was still grinning a half-hour later when I stood in front of the cameras and lights and all those newshawks who were quivering like a pack of hounds about to be turned loose after a fox. They never forgave me that grin, even though I've tried time and again to explain why they were wrong about it.

I said my piece: "Ladies and gentlemen, the President of the United States."

The news people gaped in unaccustomed silence as John, Jeffrey and Joshua strode into the room in perfect step.

DEL REY

TERRY CARR COVERS THE 70's IN SCIENCE FICTION

"As anthologies go, Terry Carr's best SF-ers are among the few in the upper echelon." —SF Review

☐ **THE BEST SCIENCE FICTION OF THE YEAR #1**   24922   1.95
Featuring Arthur C. Clarke, Norman Spinrad, Alexei Panshin. Philip José Farmer and others.

☐ **THE BEST SCIENCE FICTION OF THE YEAR #2**   24969   1.95
Featuring Robert Silverberg, Gene Wolfe, Frederik Pohl, S. M. Kornbluth and others.

☐ **THE BEST SCIENCE FICTION OF THE YEAR #3**   25015   1.95
Featuring Harlan Ellison, Vonda McIntyre, Jack Vance, R. A. Lafferty and others.

☐ **THE BEST SCIENCE FICTION OF THE YEAR #4**   24529   1.95
Featuring Larry Niven, Ursula LeGuin, William Tenn, Roger Zelazny and others.

☐ **THE BEST SCIENCE FICTION OF THE YEAR #5**   25064   1.95
Featuring Cordwainer Smith, Algis Budrys, John Varley, Gregory Benford and others.

☐ **THE BEST SCIENCE FICTION OF THE YEAR #6**   25758   1.95
Featuring Isaac Asimov, Fritz Leiber, George R. R. Martin, John Varley and others.

BB Ballantine Mail Sales
Dept. LE, 201 E. 50th Street
New York, New York 10022

Please send me the books I have checked above. I am enclosing
$........................ (please add 50¢ to cover postage and handling).
Send check or money order—no cash or C.O.D.'s please.

Name_____

Address_____

City_____State_____ Zip_____

Please allow 4 weeks for delivery.
Available at your bookstore or use this coupon.

L-9

DEL REY

ARTHUR C. CLARKE
A PASSPORT TO THE FAR REACHES OF THE UNIVERSE.

____**IMPERIAL EARTH**   25352 1.95

A visionary adventure into a fantastic future! "Clarke at the height of his powers."—*The New York Times* (A Del Rey Book)

____**CHILDHOOD'S END**   25806 1.75

The classic novel that has turned countless readers into sf devotees. "In *Childhood's End*, Arthur C. Clarke joins . . . the very small group of writers who have used science fiction as a vehicle of philosophic ideas."—*The New York Times*

____**EARTHLIGHT**   25193 1.50

A vivid and realistic novel of the future where the discovery of essential metals on the Moon brings the threat of a devastating war.

____**EXPEDITION TO EARTH**   25587 1.50

A marvelous collection of 11 short stories by the master story-teller — including "The Sentinel," the original basis for *2001: A Space Odyssey.*

____**PRELUDE TO SPACE**   25820 1.50

Mankind stands on the threshold of the universe in this compelling story of the launching of Prometheus—Earth's first true spaceship—and of the men who made it happen.

____**REACH FOR TOMORROW**   25819 1.50

A dozen Clarke stories from "Rescue Party" to "Jupiter Five." "All written with the sense of style one has come to expect from Clarke."—*The New York Times*

____**RENDEZVOUS WITH RAMA**   25288 1.95

Winner of the Hugo, Nebula and John W. Campbell Awards. "Story-telling of the highest order . . . perpetual surprise . . . breathless suspense."—*The New York Times*

____**TALES FROM THE WHITE HART**   25746 1.50

A sparkling collection of fifteen hilarious tales — including "Moving Spirit," "The Reluctant Orchid," and "The Defenestration of Ermintrude Inch."

BB Ballantine Mail Sales
Dept. LE, 201 E. 50th Street
New York, New York 10022

Please send me the books I have checked above. I am enclosing
$........................ (please add 50¢ to cover postage and handling).
Send check or money order—no cash or C.O.D.'s please.

Name_____

Address_____

City_____ State_____ Zip_____

Please allow 4 weeks for delivery.

L-24